Emily Brontë

Wuthering Heights

Retold by **Maud Jackson**
Activities by **Justin Rainey**
Illustrated by **Duilio Lopez**

Editor: Emma Berridge
Design and art direction: Nadia Maestri
Computer graphics: Simona Corniola
Picture research: Laura Lagomarsino

© 2006   Black Cat Publishing,
           an imprint of Cideb Editrice, Genoa, Canterbury

Picture credits:
By courtesy of the National Portrait Gallery, London: 4; UNITED
ARTISTS/Album: 5; © Leslie Garland Picture Library/Alamy: 97.

We would be happy to receive your comments and suggestions, and give
you any other information concerning our material.
editorial@blackcat-cideb.com
www.blackcat-cideb.com
www.cideb.it

CISQ CISQ CERT
TEXTBOOKS AND
TEACHING MATERIALS
The quality of the publisher's
design, production and sales processes has
been certified to the standard of
UNI EN ISO 9001

ISBN 978-88-530-0569-4 Book   ISBN 88-530-0569-6
ISBN 978-88-530-0568-7 Book + CD   ISBN 88-530-0568-8

Printed in Italy by Litoprint, Genoa

Contents

CAE   Cambridge Certificate in Advanced English-style exercises

T: GRADE 9   Trinity-style exercises (Grade 9)

Chapters 2, 3, 4, 8, 13, 15 and 18 are recorded.

These symbols indicate the beginning and end of the extracts linked to the listening activities.

The Brontë Sisters by Patrick Branwell Brontë (1817-48).

Emily Brontë
and Wuthering Heights

In the 1820s and 30s, three remarkable sisters – Charlotte, Emily and Anne Brontë – grew up at the parsonage [1] of Howarth, a desolate village on the Yorkshire moors. [2] This physical isolation was compensated by the extent of their reading: they had access to their father's large library and were deeply influenced by their reading there, which included the Bible and the works of Homer, Virgil, Shakespeare, Milton, Byron and Scott. After their mother's death in

1. **parsonage** : parson's (vicar's) house.
2. **moors** : open areas of hilly countryside covered with rough grass.

1821, their aunt came to live with them. Her severe Calvinist views – expressed in tales of hell and divine punishment – made a lasting impression on the girls.

In 1846 a volume of poems by Charlotte, Emily and Anne appeared under the title *Poems by Currer, Ellis and Acton Bell*. The decision to use male pseudonyms had been made because of Emily's reluctance to publish under her own name. The following year, Charlotte's *Jane Eyre*, Emily's *Wuthering Heights* and Anne's *Agnes Grey* were

A scene from the 1939 film of **Wuthering Heights**,
starring Laurence Olivier and Merle Oberon.

published. Emily died of tuberculosis in 1848; she was only thirty years old.

Wuthering Heights is one of the most powerful novels ever written. Set in the desolate windswept [1] landscape in which Emily Brontë spent her life, it is a story of passion and hatred, jealousy and revenge, religious fear and superstition. As such, it has much more in common with the Gothic novel, which preceded it, than with the more typically Victorian works of Dickens, Thackeray and George Eliot. For example, Victorian protagonists are usually good – or at least they wish to be good. By contrast, the protagonists of *Wuthering Heights* – Heathcliff and Catherine – have no interest in being good. They wish rather to live life to the fullest, to satisfy their various volcanic desires. They are fascinating and compelling, but their attraction does not depend on goodness or even on reason: both are frequently nasty, possibly evil and probably mad. Despite or perhaps because of this, we read on, gripped [2] by their story.

1 **Answer the questions below.**

1 What did the Brontës' father do?
2 What two facts influenced the sisters' creative imagination?
3 Why is 1847 a significant year in Emily Brontë's life?
4 What was Emily Brontë's pseudonym?
5 How was *Wuthering Heights* different from later Victorian novels?
6 Where does the fascination of Catherine and Heathcliff lie?
7 Which word in the following lists is different, and why?
   A windswept/jealous/bleak/isolated
   B Shakespeare/Milton/Scott/Dickens
   C Emily/Acton/Ellis/Currer

---

1. **windswept** : exposed to strong winds.
2. **gripped** : (here) absorbed.

The Characters

Catherine Earnshaw

Heathcliff

Catherine Linton

Isabella Linton

Hindley Earnshaw

Hareton Earnshaw

Linton Heathcliff

Edgar Linton

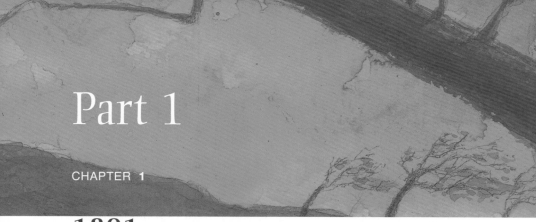

Part 1

1801. I have just returned from a visit to my landlord, [1] who is my only neighbour. This is certainly a beautiful place! In all England, there is nowhere so completely removed from the stir [2] of society. It is a misanthropist's heaven, and Mr Heathcliff and I are a suitable pair to divide the desolation between us. A fine fellow! [3] His black eyes looked at me suspiciously, and he did not offer to shake my hand. I am interested to meet a man who seems even more reserved than I am.

'Mr Heathcliff? I am Mr Lockwood, your new tenant [4] at Thrushcross Grange.'

'Come in,' he replied reluctantly, as if he really wanted to say, 'Go to the devil!'

As I followed him into the house, he called out, 'Joseph! Take Mr Lockwood's horse and then bring us some wine.'

So, I thought, this Joseph is the only servant in the house. No wonder the grass is growing between the paving stones, with no one to cut it but the cows.

Mr Heathcliff's house is called Wuthering Heights. It is a sturdy [5] stone house with narrow windows set deep in the walls.

---

1. **landlord** : person who rents his property to someone for money.
2. **stir** : action, movement.
3. **fellow** : man.
4. **tenant** : person who rents property from someone for money.
5. **sturdy** : strong and solid.

'Wuthering' is an adjective used only by the people of this region, meaning 'windy' or 'stormy', and indeed the house is built on top of a hill and is completely exposed to the north wind. The few stunted [1] trees and thorn bushes around it all slant [2] in one direction. Around the door of Wuthering Heights are grotesque carvings, and over it the date '1500' and the name 'Hareton Earnshaw' are inscribed. I wanted to ask Mr Heathcliff to tell me the history of the place, but he seemed so very unfriendly that I decided against it.

The door opens straight into the sitting room. At one end of the room is a large oak dresser, [3] its shelves crowded with pewter [4] dishes and silver tankards. [5] Legs of beef, ham, and mutton hang from the wooden beams [6] of the ceiling. Above the fireplace, various guns are attached to the wall as ornaments. The floor is of smooth white stone, and the hard wooden chairs are painted green or black. In one corner a female hunting dog lay surrounded by her puppies, and other dogs lurked [7] in the shadows.

Mr Heathcliff himself looks like a dark-skinned gypsy with the dress and manners of a gentleman, a little untidy perhaps, but with a tall handsome figure. Some people might think him proud, but I think his reserve — like mine — is probably the result of an aversion to displays of feeling. He'll love and hate in secret and be almost angry if anyone loves or hates him in return. No, perhaps I am assuming too much. Perhaps the reasons for Mr

1. **stunted** : small in height.
2. **slant** : incline.
3. **dresser** : piece of furniture with shelves above and drawers or cupboards below.
4. **pewter** : grey metal.
5. **tankards** : containers out of which beer is drunk.
6. **beams** : long, thick pieces of wood.
7. **lurked** : hid.

Heathcliff's reserve are different from my own. Let us hope that there is no one else quite like me. My dear mother used to say that I would never have a comfortable home, and only last summer I proved myself perfectly unworthy of one.

While enjoying a month of fine weather at the sea-coast, I met a fascinating young lady and fell in love with her. I never told her that I loved her, but I suppose she guessed from the way I looked at her. She began to look lovingly at me, and what did I do? I confess with shame that I became cold and distant. I retired into my shell, like a snail. The young lady thought that she had made a terrible mistake. She was confused and embarrassed, so she left the place immediately. Behaviour such as this has given me a reputation for heartlessness, but I am not heartless.

I took a seat by Mr Heathcliff's fireplace, and he sat opposite me. I tried to stroke[1] the hunting dog, but she growled[2] at me.

'You had better leave the dog alone,' growled Mr Heathcliff. Then he went to the cellar in search of Joseph, leaving me surrounded by his ill-tempered dogs, who watched my every movement.

Anxious not to be bitten, I kept still, but, to vent[3] my feelings, I whispered, 'Keep away, you savage curs!'[4] This provoked an attack. Four dogs leapt on me at once, snarling[5] and baring[6] their teeth. I snatched up[7] the poker[8] to defend myself and cried out for help.

1. **stroke** : caress.
2. **growled** : made an angry sound typical of dogs.
3. **vent** : give voice to.
4. **curs** : (here) aggressive dogs.
5. **snarling** : making angry sounds typical of dogs.
6. **baring** : showing.
7. **snatched up** : quickly picked up.
8. **poker** : metal stick used to move the wood in the fireplace.

Mr Heathcliff and Joseph appeared at the door but made no effort to save me. Fortunately a big strong woman from the kitchen rushed to my aid. She shouted at the dogs and hit them with a frying pan, until they let go of me.

'What the devil is the matter?' asked Mr Heathcliff.

'What the devil indeed!' I replied. 'You should not leave a stranger alone with those dogs, sir. They are as savage as tigers.'

'They are hunting dogs, not pets. Have a glass of wine.'

'No, thank you.'

'Did they bite you?'

'If they had, I would have killed them!'

Mr Heathcliff grinned. 'Come, come,'[1] he said. 'Calm down, Mr Lockwood. Here, take a little wine. Guests are so rare in this house that my dogs and I don't know how to receive them. Your health, sir!'

I raised my glass to his and replied, 'And yours.' It would have been foolish to take offence at the behaviour of dogs. Besides, Mr Heathcliff was amused by my distress,[2] and I did not want to give him any more amusement.

Mr Heathcliff relaxed a little and began to tell me about the advantages and disadvantages of Thrushcross Grange. I enjoyed my conversation with him, and offered to visit again tomorrow. He did not seem to like the idea, but I will go anyway. He makes me feel like a sociable man, compared with him.

1. **come, come** : relax.
2. **distress** : suffering.

Go back to the text

1 Lockwood meets Heathcliff for the first time. He is in a similar position to us, the reader. He makes assumptions about new people that enter his life. What assumptions does he make about Heathcliff?

2 Everything about the house is unfriendly, even the name! What events make Lockwood feel unwelcome?

3 What vocabulary communicates the threatening nature of the dogs?

4 'Guests are so rare in this house that my dogs and I don't know how to receive them.' What can you guess about life at Wuthering Heights from this?

5 We will see that *Wuthering Heights* contains several contrasts. Mr Lockwood notices that Heathcliff is a man of contrasts. Complete these three contrasting pairs that appear in Chapter One, then find two examples in the text.

Positive	Negative
A love	
B	rudeness
C gentleman	

6 What similarity does Lockwood notice between himself and Heathcliff?

7 The following day Lockwood returns to Wuthering Heights and meets other residents of the house.

1 Which of them do you think will play an important part in the story? Discuss your ideas with a partner.

2 What negative features do some of these characters have in common with Heathcliff?

Yesterday afternoon, when I left Thrushcross Grange, it was misty and cold. I had wanted to stay by the fire in my study, but when I went in I found no fire there. The maid [1] was cleaning the fireplace. So I set out and walked four miles through the mud to Wuthering Heights. When I got to Heathcliff's door, a few feathery snowflakes were falling. No one answered my knock: though I knocked loudly, the only result was that the dogs inside began to howl. [2] Then Joseph put his head out of the barn [3] window. He was an old man with a sour [4] expression. 'What do you want?' he shouted. 'The master's in the fields with the sheep. You will have to go there, if you want to speak to him.'

'Is there no one inside to open the door?' I shouted back.

'No one but the mistress, and she would not open the door if you knocked all night.'

I was surprised to hear there was a mistress at Wuthering Heights. 'Can't you tell her who I am, Joseph?'

'No,' he replied, and his head vanished.

The snow was falling thickly by this time. I tried to open the door, but it did not move. Then a young man with a pitchfork [5] on his shoulder appeared in the yard. [6] He beckoned to me, and I

---

1. **maid** : female servant.
2. **howl** : make a long crying sound.
3. **barn** : large building on a farm used to keep things in.
4. **sour** : (here) unfriendly.
5. **pitchfork** : big fork with a long handle used on a farm.
6. **yard** : area of land next to a building covered with a hard surface.

followed him around the house to another door. Finally I reached the huge, warm, cheerful sitting room. There was an immense fire in the fireplace. The table was laid for the evening meal, and near the table sat the mistress.

I bowed [1] and waited, thinking she would ask me to sit down, but she just looked at me in silence. 'Rough weather!' I remarked. She did not reply. I stared at her and she at me. I felt very uncomfortable.

'Sit down,' said the young man gruffly. [2] 'He'll be in soon.'

The female hunting dog — whose name was Juno — moved the tip of her tail as if to greet me. 'A beautiful animal!' I said, trying once more to engage the mistress in conversation. 'Will you give away the puppies, Mrs Heathcliff, or keep them?'

'They are not mine,' she replied, in a voice even colder than Heathcliff's.

'Ah? Well.' I decided to try the weather again. 'It's very cold out this evening.'

'You should have stayed at home.'

She was a slender and very young woman. Her figure and face were lovely. Her golden curls hung loose on her shoulders, and her eyes would have been irresistible had their expression been pleasant. Fortunately for my susceptible heart, their expression was a combination of scorn [3] and desperation that seemed most unnatural in a beautiful young woman.

She stood and reached up to take a jar of tea from one of the

---

1.   **bowed** : bent my head as a sign of respect.
2.   **gruffly** : in an unfriendly way.
3.   **scorn** : lack of respect for someone or something.

shelves. I rose to get it for her, but she snapped [1] at me, 'I don't want your help. I can get it myself.'

'I beg your pardon.'

'Were you asked to tea?' she demanded, putting a spoonful of tea in the pot.

'I would like a cup,' I answered.

'Were you asked?' she repeated.

'No,' I said, smiling. 'You are the proper person to ask me.'

She stopped preparing the tea and sat down in her chair again, clearly angry.

The young man came and stood in front of the fire, glancing [2] at me from time to time with a stern [3] look, as if I were his worst enemy. At first I had thought he was a servant, but now I was not so sure. His dress and speech were both rough, not at all like those of Mr and Mrs Heathcliff. His thick brown hair was wild and messy, [4] and he was unshaven. His hands were brown like those of a common labourer. Yet there was something proud and free about him.

I felt relieved when Heathcliff came in. 'You see I have come to visit you again, as I promised,' I said cheerfully. 'I won't be able to leave for half an hour because of this snow. I hope you don't mind me staying that long.'

'Half an hour?' he said, shaking the snow from his clothes. 'The snow will not stop in half an hour. Why do you go out walking in a snowstorm? You could get lost. Even people who

---

1. **snapped** : said in a short and unfriendly way.
2. **glancing** : looking quickly.
3. **stern** : severe.
4. **messy** : untidy.

know the moors well sometimes get lost in snowy weather.'

'Perhaps one of your servants could show me the way back to Thrushcross Grange?'

'Certainly not.'

'Well, then, I must try to find the way alone.'

The shabby [1] young man turned to the mistress and said, 'Are you going to make the tea?'

'Is he having tea with us?' she asked Heathcliff, pointing at me.

'Get it ready, will you?' was the answer, spoken so savagely that I started. The tone in which the words were said revealed a genuine bad nature. I no longer thought that Heathcliff was a fine fellow.

'Now, sir,' he said to me, 'bring your chair forward,' and we all sat down to tea, including the rustic youth. We ate in silence.

I thought it was my presence that made them so grim [2] and taciturn. Surely they were not like that all the time. So I tried to make cheerful conversation to alleviate the mood. 'Many people would think a life of such seclusion could not be a happy one, Mr Heathcliff, but I am sure that here, surrounded by your family, with your amiable lady...'

'My amiable lady!' he interrupted, with an almost diabolical sneer [3] on his face. 'Where is my amiable lady?'

'I mean Mrs Heathcliff, your wife.'

'Do you think that her spirit is with me in Wuthering Heights, even though her body is gone?'

1. **shabby** : dirty, untidy.
2. **grim** : very serious.
3. **sneer** : sign of contempt.

I realised that I had made a mistake, and I tried to correct it. I should have seen that there was too great a difference of age between them: he was about forty; she looked no more than seventeen. At forty a man does not think that a girl would marry him for love. That dream is the comfort of our old age.

I suddenly thought that the clown beside me, who was drinking his tea out of a bowl and eating with unwashed hands, might be her husband. He might be Heathcliff junior. What a pity! She must have married him out of ignorance that better men existed. I thought, I must be careful not to make her regret her choice. The last reflection may seem conceited; it was not. The young man seemed to me almost repulsive. I knew, through experience, that I was quite attractive.

'Mrs Heathcliff is my daughter-in-law,' said Heathcliff. He looked at her with a peculiar expression on his face. He seemed to hate her.

'Ah, certainly — I see now. You are the happy husband of the amiable lady,' I said, turning to the young man.

This was worse than before. The youth blushed [1] a deep red and clenched [2] his fist as though he were about to hit me.

'Neither of us is married to her. Her husband is dead,' said Heathcliff. 'She was married to my son.'

'And this young man is...?'

'Certainly not my son!' Heathcliff smiled.

'My name is Hareton Earnshaw,' growled the other. 'And you must treat it with respect!'

'I've shown no disrespect,' was my reply. I began to feel very out of place in this family circle. The dismal atmosphere outweighed the physical comforts around me, and I thought I would not come again. When tea was over, I went to the window to examine the weather. It was not a pleasant sight: darkness was falling, and the wind was full of swirling [3] snow. 'I don't think I will be able to get home without a guide,' I said.

'Hareton, bring those sheep into the barn,' said Heathcliff.

'What shall I do?' I asked, with rising irritation. I turned to look at Heathcliff, but I found that the only other people in the room were Joseph and Mrs Heathcliff. Joseph was feeding the dogs. Mrs Heathcliff was entertaining herself by burning matches in the fire.

'How can you stand there idle,' [4] said Joseph to Mrs Heathcliff,

1. **blushed** : became red in the face from embarrassment.
2. **clenched** : closed tightly.
3. **swirling** : moving in twists and turns.
4. **idle** : not doing anything.

'when everyone else is working? But you are nothing, and it's no use talking. You'll never improve: you'll go to the devil just like your mother!'

I thought for a moment that he was talking to me, and I stepped forward, intending to kick the old rascal, but I stopped when I heard Mrs Heathcliff's reply. 'You old hypocrite! Aren't you afraid that the devil will come and take you away for speaking his name? You leave me alone, or I'll ask him to do it!' She took a long dark book from a shelf. 'I am learning witchcraft, [1] Joseph — the Black Art. Soon I will get rid of you all by black magic. The red cow didn't die by chance, and your rheumatism is no accident!'

'Oh, wicked, wicked!' cried the old man, hurrying out of the room. 'May the Lord save us from evil!'

'Mrs Heathcliff,' I said, when he was gone, 'is there no one in the house who would guide me back to Thrushcross Grange?'

'Nobody,' she said.

'Then I will have to stay here.'

Heathcliff appeared in the doorway, looking grim. 'I hope this will be a lesson to you to take no more walks in the snow. You say you will have to stay here. Well, then you must share a bed with Hareton or Joseph. I have no guest rooms.'

'I can sleep in a chair in this room,' I replied.

'I don't want a stranger in my house while I'm sleeping,' said Heathcliff.

With this insult, my patience was at an end. I pushed past him and went out into the yard, just as Hareton was coming in. It was so dark, I could not see the gate.

1. **witchcraft** : the use of magic powers, especially evil ones.

'I'll go with him as far as the park,' said Hareton to Heathcliff.

'You'll go with him to hell!' cried Heathcliff. 'Who will look after the horses if you go?'

'A man's life is more important,' said Mrs Heathcliff, more kindly than I had expected.

'I won't save his life for you!' said Hareton. 'If you care about him, you had better be quiet!'

'Well, if he dies, I hope his ghost will haunt you, and I hope that Mr Heathcliff never finds another tenant, and that Thrushcross Grange goes to ruin!'

'Listen! She's cursing them!' muttered Joseph. He was milking the cows by the light of a lantern. I took the lantern and quickly went out through the gate, saying that I would send it back tomorrow.

'Master! Master! He's stealing the lantern!' cried Joseph. 'Let the dogs go after him!'

Two hairy monsters leapt at my throat. They knocked me down, and the light was extinguished. My nose began to bleed. I heard Hareton and Heathcliff laughing. Trembling with rage and humiliation, I cursed them. My threats of retaliation sounded like King Lear's, [1] but still Heathcliff laughed. Finally the big strong woman who had saved me from the dogs on my first visit came out to see what was happening. Her name is Zillah. 'Well, Mr Earnshaw,' she cried. 'Are you going to murder the gentleman in our own back yard? Come, come, sir. You are bleeding. I'll take care of you.'

She poured a pint of icy water down my neck to stop the bleeding. Then Heathcliff told her to give me a glass of brandy and prepare a bed for me.

1. **King Lear's** : reference to Shakespeare's King Lear, whose threats of retaliation have no effect.

Go back to the text

1 Prepare for the complicated family relationships that exist in *Wuthering Heights*! Revise family relations. Who is your:

1 son's wife?   *your daughter-in-law*
2 son's son?
3 mother's brother?
4 brother's daughter?
5 mother's brother's son?

2 Lockwood's confusion about the inhabitants of Wuthering Heights is similar to ours. He makes assumptions that are later proved wrong.

1 What mistakes does he make regarding Heathcliff's family?
2 What relations really exist between the 'amiable lady', Hareton and Heathcliff?

3 Put these events from Chapter Two into their correct order.

A ☐ Lockwood has tea with Heathcliff, the young lady and Hareton.
B ☐ Lockwood tries to leave the house and is attacked by the dogs.
C ☐ Heathcliff tells Lockwood that the snow will last for more than half an hour.

4 'An atmosphere of madness and menace dominates the house and common civility is abandoned.' Find evidence of this in the behaviour of the following inhabitants.

1 Mrs Heathcliff: ....
2 Heathcliff: ....
3 Hareton: ....
4 Joseph: ....

5 Go back and listen to Lockwood's attempts to make conversation with the inhabitants of Wuthering Heights. How does his tone of voice differ from the others'?

As she led me upstairs to the room she had chosen for me, Zillah told me to be very quiet and hide the candle, because her master never let anyone stay in that room.

I asked the reason, but she said she did not know. She had only lived in the house a year or two, she said. So many strange things went on in the house that she no longer asked about them.

When I was alone in the room, I looked around. The only furniture was a chair, a wardrobe, and a large oak case with windows in it, like a carriage. I looked inside it and found a bed, and, above the bed, a window. On the window sill [1] was a pile of books. I opened the door of the oak case and climbed in with my candle. When I had shut the door behind me, I felt safe from Heathcliff or anyone else.

As I placed my candle on the window sill, I noticed that it was covered with writing, scratched [2] in the paint. It was a name repeated in all kinds of letters, large and small — 'Catherine Earnshaw', sometimes changing to 'Catherine Heathcliff' or 'Catherine Linton'.

Feeling sleepy, I leaned my head against the window, and read and reread the names until my eyes closed; but then I saw white letters like ghosts in the dark, and the air swarmed [3] with

---

1. **sill** : piece of wood or stone forming the base of a window or a door.
2. **scratched** : (here) written, cut.
3. **swarmed** : (here) was full.

Catherines. I woke up and realised that my candle was starting to burn the cover of one of the books. I opened the book. It was a Bible. The name 'Catherine Earnshaw' was written on the fly-leaf [1] with a date of twenty-five years ago. I looked at all the other books one by one. Catherine's library was well chosen and well used, but the books had not been used in the usual way. She had written a diary in the margins of the books: every bit of blank [2] space left by the printer was filled with Catherine's childish handwriting. On one page I found, to my delight, an excellent caricature of Joseph. I began to feel a keen interest for the unknown Catherine and so read a little of her diary:

'An awful Sunday! I wish my father were back again. Hindley is being horrible to Heathcliff. H. and I are going to rebel. We began this evening. Joseph had made us listen while he gave a sermon [3] three hours long! When we came down, Hindley said, "What? Have you finished already?" He had been enjoying himself by the fire, kissing Frances and talking nonsense. H. and I were going to play, but Joseph said. "Shame on you! Your father was only buried yesterday, and you want to play! You are evil children. Sit down and read a good book and think of your souls!" He gave me a pious text to read, but I picked it up and threw it into the dog-kennel, and I told him I hated a good book. Heathcliff kicked his book into the same place. Then what a fuss! [4] "Master Hindley!" cried Joseph. "Look what those evil

1. **fly-leaf** : empty page at the beginning or end of a book.
2. **blank** : empty.
3. **sermon** : long moral talk.
4. **fuss** : show of dissatisfaction.

children have done!" Heathcliff says that we should steal some food and go running on the moors and stay there all day. I like the idea. We cannot be damper [1] or colder out there in the rain than we are here.'

I suppose they did go, for the next sentence was on a new subject: 'Hindley has made me cry so much that my head aches. Poor Heathcliff! Hindley calls him a vagabond and won't let him sit with us or eat with us anymore. He says that I must not play with Heathcliff. If I do, he says, he will throw Heathcliff out of the house. He blames our father (how dare he?) for treating Heathcliff too liberally. Hindley swears that he will reduce Heathcliff to his right place.'

I began to feel sleepy once more, and my eye wandered from manuscript to print. At the top of the page it said, 'Seventy Times Seven and the First of the Seventy-First. A Pious Discourse by the Reverend Jabes Branderham.' I must have fallen asleep then.

What can explain the terrible dream I had? It must have been the result of poor digestion or bad temper. I dreamt that it was morning, and I was going home through the snow, with Joseph as my guide. He kept telling me that I should have brought a pilgrim's staff, [2] that I would never get into the house without one. He waved his thick walking stick at me proudly, and so I understood that was what he meant by 'pilgrim's staff'. At first I thought it absurd that I should need such a weapon to get into my own house; but then I realised that we were going to hear the

---

1. **damper** : slightly wetter.
2. **staff** : long stick.

famous Jabes Branderham preach a sermon on 'The Seventy Times Seven'.

We came to the chapel. I have passed it really in my walks; it is a damp, gloomy, [1] dilapidated place. However, in my dream, Jabes preached — good God — what a sermon! It was divided into four hundred and ninety parts, each as long as a normal sermon and each discussing a different sin! Some of these were sins I had never thought about before. In my dream I was terribly tired and bored by the sermon. Finally, I rose to my feet and accused Jabes of the sin that no Christian need pardon — the sin of boring us all to death. But Jabes turned to me and accused me of The First of the Seventy-First! He called upon his congregation to execute the Lord's judgement upon me. With that, the entire congregation attacked me with their pilgrim's staffs. I tried to take Joseph's staff from him, so I could defend myself, but the old man was too strong for me...

At that point — much to my relief — I woke up. The branch of a tree was tapping [2] against the window in the wind. I went back to sleep and dreamt even more disagreeably than before, if that is possible. I dreamt I was awake in the oak case. I could hear the wind outside and the tapping of the branch. The tapping annoyed me so much that I decided to stop it. I tried to open the window, but could not. I broke the glass with my fist and stretched [3] my hand out to break off the branch, but instead my fingers closed around a little ice-cold hand!

---

1. **gloomy** : dark and depressing.
2. **tapping** : hitting lightly.
3. **stretched** : put out my hand as far as possible.

The intense horror of nightmare overcame me. I tried to withdraw my arm, but the little hand clung [1] to me, and a most melancholy voice sobbed, 'Let me in! Let me in!'

'Who are you?' I asked, still struggling to free myself.

'Catherine Linton,' replied the voice. (Why did I think of Linton? I had read Earnshaw twenty times for every Linton.) 'I have come home. I was lost on the moor!'

In the darkness, I could see a child's face, looking through the window. Terror made me cruel, and, since I could not free my arm from its grip, [2] I pulled its wrist onto the broken glass of the window and rubbed [3] it back and forth until blood ran down and soaked [4] the bedclothes. Still it cried, 'Let me in!' and maintained its grip.

'How can I? Let me go if you want me to let you in.'

The fingers relaxed. I snatched my hand back through the hole, piled the books up in front of it, and stopped [5] my ears so that I would not hear those dreadful [6] cries.

'Go away!' I shouted. 'I will not let you in, not if you beg for twenty years.'

'It is twenty years,' cried the voice. 'I've been a lost child for twenty years!'

Then I heard a faint scratching outside, and the pile of books moved forwards, as though pushed from behind. I screamed aloud.

1. **clung** : held tightly.
2. **grip** : (here) hold.
3. **rubbed** : moved with force.
4. **soaked** : made very wet.
5. **stopped** : (here) blocked, put my hands over.
6. **dreadful** : terrible.

Unfortunately, the scream was real. Someone ran into my bedroom. I saw his light flickering, [1] but he could not see me. 'Is anyone here?' he whispered. I recognised Heathcliff's voice, and thought it best to confess my presence at once, so I opened the door of the oak case to get out. The first creak of the door opening startled him like an electric shock. He dropped his candle and had difficulty picking it up again. 'It is only your guest, sir', I said, wishing to spare him the humiliation of showing his cowardice further. 'I had a terrible nightmare and screamed in my sleep. I'm sorry I disturbed you.'

'Oh, the devil take you, Mr Lockwood!' cried Heathcliff, putting his candle down on a chair because his hand was shaking. 'Who put you in this room?' he asked, crushing [2] his fingernails into his palms and grinding [3] his teeth, to stop the trembling. 'Who was it? I'll throw them out of the house!'

'It was your servant Zillah,' I replied, 'and she deserves to be thrown out. She must have known that the place was haunted. It is swarming with ghosts!'

'Well, go back to bed Mr Lockwood. But don't scream again. Nothing could excuse that noise unless you were having your throat cut!'

'If the little devil had got in through the window, she probably would have strangled me!'

'Who do you mean?' asked Heathcliff.

'Catherine Earnshaw or Catherine Linton or whatever her

---

1. **flickering** : burning or shinning in an unsteady way.
2. **crushing** : (here) forcing.
3. **grinding** : (here) moving together noisily.

name was. She told me she had been walking on the moors for twenty years, the wicked little soul!'

'How dare you talk that way to me!' thundered Heathcliff savagely. 'God! He is mad to speak so!' And he struck his forehead with rage.

At first I felt offended by this, but then I took pity on him — he seemed so powerfully affected — and told him more about my dream. Meanwhile, he sat in the oak case, so that I could no longer see his face, but I could tell from his breathing and the movement of his arm's shadow on the wall that he was weeping.

'Mr Lockwood,' he said at last, 'go and wait for me in the corridor.'

I went out of the room, but then stopped, for the corridor was dark. He thought I had gone, otherwise he never would have done what he did next: he broke the window open, bursting into tears as he did so. 'Come in! Come in!' he sobbed. 'Cathy, do come! Oh do — once more! Oh! My heart's darling! Hear me this time, Catherine, at last!'

The ghost, however, gave no sign, and the wind and the snow swirled in through the window and blew out the light.

Go back to the text

1 The mystery continues and Lockwood, like us, is confused by the three Catherines. Which of the following questions can you answer by the end of Chapter Three? Two (0 and 00) have been done for you.

  0 Where did Lockwood sleep?
In a large oak case like a carriage.

00 What is the relationship between Catherine Earnshaw, Catherine Heathcliff and Catherine Linton?
We don't know.

  1 Whose Bible did Lockwood read?

  2 When were the diary entries written?

  3 Who are Hindley and Frances?

  4 Is Catherine's father alive?

  5 What feelings exist between Hindley and Heathcliff?

  6 How would Catherine and Heathcliff like to spend their days?

2 Lockwood has two dreams. Which do you think will be the most important in the story: A or B?

  A 'The entire congregation attacked me with their pilgrim's staffs'

  B 'I've been a lost child for twenty years!'

3 What does Heathcliff's reaction to Lockwood's dream tell you about his feelings for Catherine?

4 As readers we make assumptions about characters we meet, just as we do in real life. We try and create meaning by assuming relations and connections between people and events. We cannot yet answer all the questions in exercise 1. In small groups make suppositions; compare your ideas and make a note of them. As the story develops check if you were right.

5 In the next chapter, Mrs Dean, Lockwood's housekeeper, tells him (and us) about her life as a young woman at Wuthering Heights. What makes Heathcliff different from the others at Wuthering Heights?

CHAPTER 4

The next morning, Heathcliff walked with me to the gate of Thrushcross Grange. From there it was only two miles to the house, but I managed to get lost among the trees, and more than once I fell in the snow. When, finally, I reached the house, I was cold and wet. My housekeeper [1] Mrs Dean met me at the door and told me that dry clothes and a fire were awaiting me in my room. All that day I stayed in my room alone, and I confess I felt rather lonely, even though I had deliberately chosen the place for its solitude. When Mrs Dean brought me my supper, I asked her to keep me company while I ate it. I sincerely hoped that she was a talkative woman.

'How long have you lived at Thrushcross Grange, Mrs Dean?'

'Eighteen years, sir. I came when the mistress married.'

'And why does your master not live here? It is a far grander [2] house than Wuthering Heights.'

'He does not like to spend money, sir. He's as rich as can be, but he never misses a chance to get richer still, even though he has no family to leave it to.'

'He told me he had a son.'

'His son is dead, sir. The young lady, Mrs Heathcliff, is his widow.'

'Where did she come from originally?' I asked.

1. **housekeeper** : person who is paid to look after a house for someone.
2. **grander** : more elegant.

'Why, here, sir! She is my late master's daughter. Her maiden name [1] was Catherine Linton. I took care of her when she was a baby, poor thing.'

I started at the name, but the next moment I realised that she could not be my ghostly Catherine.

'Yes, her father, Mr Edgar Linton, lived here before you, sir. Heathcliff was married to Mr Linton's sister. Then Cathy married her cousin, Heathcliff's son. Have you been to Wuthering Heights, sir?'

'Yes.'

'Oh, how is she, sir? How is Cathy, if you don't mind me asking?'

'She looked well and very handsome, though not happy, I think.'

'I am not surprised to hear it,' said Mrs Dean. 'And what did you think of the master?'

'He seems a rough fellow, Mrs Dean. Am I right?'

'As rough as the edge [2] of a saw, and as hard as stone. It's best to avoid him, sir.'

'Do you know anything of his history?'

'It's a cuckoo's history, [3] sir,' said Mrs Dean. 'I know all about it, except where he was born, who were his parents, and how he

---

1. **maiden name** : surname before she was married.
2. **edge** : border, outside limit.
3. **a cuckoo's history** : the cuckoo lays her egg in another bird's nest. The other bird hatches the cuckoo's egg with her own eggs and feeds the cuckoo chick as if it were her own. The cuckoo chick then pushes the other baby birds out of the nest. Heathcliff, like the baby cuckoo, is fostered by a family not his own and displaces the natural heirs of that family so that finally he is master of Wuthering Heights.

got his money at first. Hareton has been cast out [1] like the baby sparrow. [2] Everyone except Hareton himself knows how he has been cheated!' [3]

'Well, Mrs Dean. It is a most intriguing story. Will you sit with me for an hour and tell me all about it?'

'Certainly, sir. Just let me get my sewing. [4] And I'll bring you some hot soup, sir. I think you have caught a chill.'

It was true: my head felt very hot and the rest of me felt cold. A few minutes later, she returned with her sewing and a steaming bowl of soup. She gave me the soup, then sat down to begin her sewing and her story.

Before I came to live here, she said, I was almost always at Wuthering Heights. My mother had nursed Mr Hindley Earnshaw — that's Hareton's father — and I had got used to playing with the children Hindley and Cathy. One fine summer morning, Mr Earnshaw, the old master, went off to Liverpool on business. After three days, he returned, late in the evening, carrying something bundled up [5] in his coat. Hindley and Cathy thought he had brought them presents, but when he opened the coat we saw a dirty, ragged, [6] black-haired child. The child was old enough to walk and talk, but when he spoke it was in some strange language that no one could understand. Mr Earnshaw said to his wife, 'We must take him as a gift from God, my dear, although he's dark enough to have come from the devil.'

1. **cast out** : sent away.
2. **sparrow** : small brown bird.
3. **cheated** : tricked, deceived.
4. **sewing** : clothes or other items being made or repaired.
5. **bundled up** : tied up like a package.
6. **ragged** : wearing old and torn clothes.

Mrs Earnshaw was furious. She wanted to throw the 'gypsy-child', as she called him, out into the street. She asked her husband if he had gone mad. Mr Earnshaw explained that he had found the child starving and homeless in the streets of Liverpool and had decided to take him home and care for him.

Hindley and Cathy then asked about their presents, but they found that Hindley's present had been broken and Cathy's had been lost on the journey home. Hindley, who was fourteen, burst into tears. Cathy spat at the gypsy-child, because she had decided it was all his fault; but her father slapped [1] her and told her she should have better manners.

Mr Earnshaw said that the gypsy-child should sleep with

1. **slapped** : hit.

the children, but Cathy and Hindley refused to sleep with him, so I left him on the stairs, hoping he would be gone by morning. In the morning, Mr Earnshaw found him sleeping on the floor outside his bedroom door.

They called him Heathcliff. It was the name of a son who had died in childhood, and he has used it ever since, both for Christian name and for surname.

A short time after Heathcliff arrived, Mrs Earnshaw fell ill and died. Mr Earnshaw was left alone with the three children. Heathcliff and Miss Cathy became great friends, but Hindley hated him and so did I. Hindley hit him, and I pinched [1] him, but he never cried. Perhaps he was used to harsh treatment. Later, when I knew him better, I stopped hating Heathcliff, and so Hindley lost his only ally. [2] Whenever Mr Earnshaw found out that Hindley had been cruel to Heathcliff, he got very angry. He was very fond of Heathcliff and believed everything the boy said. To be fair, he did not say much, and it was usually the truth. Heathcliff was clearly Mr Earnshaw's favourite.

So, from the very beginning, Heathcliff brought bad feeling into the house. Heathcliff knew the power he had over Mr Earnshaw. By the time Mr Earnshaw died, two years later, Hindley thought of his father as an oppressor and of Heathcliff as the usurper of his father's affection. He grew bitter thinking about these injuries.

For example, I remember once Mr Earnshaw bought two colts, [3] one for each of the boys. Heathcliff took the handsomer colt, but soon it became lame. [4] When Heathcliff discovered this,

1. **pinched** : pressed his skin between two fingers causing pain.
2. **ally** : (here) friend who agreed with him.
3. **colts** : young male horses.
4. **lame** : wasn't able to walk.

he said to Hindley, 'You must exchange horses with me. If you refuse, I will tell your father of the three beatings you gave me this week. I will show him my arm, which is black to the shoulder.'

Hindley put out his tongue and hit Heathcliff. 'Go away, you dog!' cried Hindley. He picked up an iron weight, used to weigh potatoes, and threatened to throw it at Heathcliff.

'Go on! Throw it!' said Heathcliff. 'And then I will tell him that you said you will throw me out of the house as soon as he dies! He will throw you out.'

Hindley threw the weight and hit Heathcliff on the chest. Heathcliff fell down but then got up immediately, breathless and pale. Had I not prevented it, he would have gone to Mr Earnshaw and shown him the mark on his chest.

'Take my colt then, gypsy!' cried Hindley. 'And I pray that you fall off it and break your neck! Be damned, you beggarly interloper! [1] You try to trick my father out of all he has, but I'll show him what you are, you devil!'

I had no trouble persuading Heathcliff to lay the blame of his bruises on the horse, so that Mr Earnshaw would not be angry with Hindley. Indeed, he complained so seldom of Hindley's treatment that I really thought he was not vindictive — but I was completely wrong, as you will hear.

---

1. **beggarly interloper** : (here) poor intruder.

Go back to the text

1 *Wuthering Heights* is a complex story for the characters and the confusion of their names (Heathcliff, Hareton, Hindley, Catherine Earnshaw, Catherine Linton) and the shifts in time.

In Chapter Four the relationships between the various characters mentioned in Catherine's Bible (Chapter Three) and by Mrs Dean are clarified. Mrs Dean gives us a lot of information before starting her story. Sort out the facts by matching the phrases in column A with an appropriate phrase from column B.

Remember that we will understand more fully the relationships as we read the story. The sentence: 'Catherine's father was Edgar Linton' is informationally correct but at this stage in the story does not mean very much.

A	B
1 Heathcliff is	A Linton
2 Heathcliff's son	B is dead
3 Heathcliff's son	C Heathcliff's son
4 Catherine's maiden name is	D Mrs Dean's master
5 Catherine's father	E lived in Thrushcross Grange
6 Edgar Linton	F married to Edgar's sister
7 Heathcliff was	G was Edgar Linton
8 Catherine married	H was married to Catherine

2 With Mrs Dean we have a change of narrator and with it a shift in time into the past. Complete the Earnshaw family tree as it was just before Heathcliff's arrival into the Earnshaw family (see page 143).

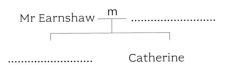

38

3 Mr Earnshaw says, 'he's dark enough to have come from the devil' and his wife calls him 'the gypsy-child'. These two images of Heathcliff dominate the story. His arrival 'from the very beginning [...] brought bad feeling into the house'. Who resented Heathcliff's presence most and why?

4 Decide whether the following statements are true or false. Correct the false ones.

	T	F
1 Mrs Dean's mother had nursed Hareton's father.	☐	☐
2 Mrs Dean rarely played with the Earnshaw children.	☐	☐
3 Only Mr Earnshaw at first acted kindly to Heathcliff.	☐	☐
4 Mrs Earnshaw died after her husband.	☐	☐

5 Who is 'he' in the following sentences: Heathcliff or Hindley?

1 He thought he had lost his place in his father's affections.

2 He usually told the truth.

3 To get what he wants, he threatens to tell Mr Earnshaw about his mistreatment.

4 He often reacted violently.

6 The sentences above provide evidence for and against both men. Put the sentences into the correct place in the table.

	For	Against
Heathcliff Hindley		

CAE 7 Work in pairs. Student A presents the case for Heathcliff, Student B presents the case for Hindley. Try to reach an agreement or 'agree to disagree'.

As Mr Earnshaw grew old and weak, Joseph gained more and more influence over him. He spoke to him about salvation and his soul. He spoke about the necessity of ruling his children rigidly. He criticised Hindley and Catherine, though he was careful not to anger him by criticising Heathcliff. Finally the master was persuaded to send Hindley away to school. I thought then there might be some peace in the house, but Catherine was still at home, and she was a wild one.

From the moment she came downstairs in the morning to the moment she went to bed at night, she caused trouble. She was always talking, singing, or laughing, and teasing [1] everyone who would not do the same. She ridiculed Joseph's religious speeches. She slapped me and told me what to do. She tormented her father by showing him how much more power she had over Heathcliff than he had. She was much too fond of Heathcliff, and the worst punishment we could give her was to keep her separate from him. Yes, she was a wild, troublesome girl, but she had the prettiest eyes and the sweetest smile I ever saw.

One evening, when the wind was howling, we all sat by the fire. Joseph was reading his Bible. I was sewing. Miss Cathy had been ill, so she was quieter than usual and leant against her father's knee. Heathcliff lay on the floor with his head in her lap. [2] I remember the master, before he fell asleep, saying, 'Why can't you always be a good girl, Cathy?'

---

1. **teasing** : making fun of.
2. **in her lap** : on her knees.

She looked up at him and laughed and said, 'Why can't you always be a good man, Father?'

But, when she saw she had offended him, she kissed his hand and said she would sing him to sleep. She sang very quietly until his head sank on his breast. We all sat silent for half and hour, not wishing to wake him, then Joseph rose and said he must wake the master: it was time for prayers and bed.

Joseph called him, but the master did not stir. Then Joseph told the children to go up to bed immediately, and I realised that something was wrong. 'I shall just kiss Father goodnight first,' said Catherine, and she put her arms around his neck before we could stop her. The poor child screamed out, 'Oh, he's dead, Heathcliff! He's dead!' They both started to cry, and I did too, but Joseph asked what there was to cry about, when the master's soul had gone straight to heaven.

Hindley came home for the funeral. He was master now. Much to everyone's surprise, he brought a wife with him. Her name was Frances. He never told us where she was born, or who her people were. She probably had no money at all. Why else would he have kept his marriage secret from his father?

She acted very strangely while the funeral was going on. She trembled and wept, and, when at last I asked her what was the matter, she said she was afraid of dying. I thought that was ridiculous. She was a bit thin but young with a fresh complexion and eyes that sparkled like diamonds. I noticed that she had trouble breathing when she climbed the stairs, and that she was nervous, and that she coughed a lot, but I did not know then what these symptoms meant.

Hindley had changed a lot in the three years of his absence. On the day he returned, he told Joseph that the servants must

stay in the kitchen from now on: we could no longer sit by the fire with the family as we used to do. Sometimes he got angry with Heathcliff and said that he too would have to eat in the kitchen with the servants. While the old master had been alive, Heathcliff had been educated like the other children, but now Hindley stopped Heathcliff's lessons and said he must work outdoors on the farm.

At first Heathcliff did not mind too much, because Cathy taught him what she learnt in her lessons, and she worked or played with him in the fields. Cathy and Heathcliff were growing up like a pair of young savages. Hindley did not care what they did or how they behaved, so long as they stayed away from him. They loved to run away to the moors together in the morning and remain there all day. They were punished for doing this — Joseph made Catherine learn passages from the Bible and thrashed[1] Heathcliff until his arm ached — but these punishments were mere things to laugh at while they were away and free on the moors.

One evening Hindley sent them out of the sitting room for making too much noise. When bedtime came, we could not find them anywhere. Hindley was furious and told us to lock the house. No one, he said, was to let them in if they returned. Joseph followed his orders, but I stayed up by the open window, listening for them, determined to let them in. It was raining outside. The poor things would be soaking wet.

After a while, I heard footsteps on the road and saw a lantern. I ran to the door to let them in, but Heathcliff was there alone. 'Where's Miss Catherine?' I asked.

---

1. **thrashed** : hit.

'At Thrushcross Grange,' he said. 'And I would be there too, but they did not invite me to stay. You see, Nelly, when Cathy and I ran away this evening, we saw the lights of Thrushcross Grange, and we wanted to see how the Lintons passed their Sunday evenings. We ran all the way from the Heights to the park without stopping. Cathy lost the race because she was barefoot. When we got to the Grange we looked in through the drawing room [1] window. It is beautiful inside: there is a red carpet and red chairs and a white ceiling with a gold border;

1. **drawing room** : room in a house where people relax and receive guests.

from the middle of the ceiling hangs a shower of glass drops shimmering [1] with little candles. Mr and Mrs Linton weren't there. Edgar and his sister had it all to themselves. Shouldn't they have been happy? We would have thought ourselves in heaven! But guess what they were doing? Isabella lay screaming at one end of the room, and Edgar stood weeping at the other. In the middle a little dog was whimpering [2] and licking its paw. They had been fighting over it and had nearly torn it in two. The idiots! How we laughed at them!'

'But you still have not told me,' I said, 'how Cathy was left behind.'

'Well, Edgar and Isabella heard us laughing, and they cried out: "Oh, Mamma! Oh, Papa! Oh!" Cathy and I decided to run away, but, as we were running, she fell. They had let the dogs loose and one of them had Cathy's ankle in its teeth! "Run, Heathcliff!" she whispered. She was not crying at all, even though it must have been very painful. I tried to open the dog's mouth to free Cathy's ankle. Just then the servants ran up. They took us to the house. Mr and Mrs Linton were horrified at the sight of us. They said I looked like a gypsy and that no doubt we were thieves. Then Edgar Linton recognised Cathy. They see us at church, you know. "Why, it's Miss Earnshaw!" he said. "Nonsense!" cried Mrs Linton. "Why would Miss Earnshaw be running around the moor barefoot with a gypsy?" But finally she believed it, and then she felt sorry that her dog had made Cathy's ankle bleed, and she called a doctor and said that Cathy must stay as her guest. But they had not the good manners to invite me to stay with her.'

1. **shimmering** : shining with a soft, unsteady light.
2. **whimpering** : crying weakly in pain.

Go back to the text

1 'From the moment she came downstairs in the morning to the moment she went to bed at night, she caused trouble.' Find examples of Catherine's wild and troublesome behaviour.

2 What changes does Hindley's return to Wuthering Heights bring?

3 Cathy and Heathcliff 'loved to run away to the moors together in the morning and remain there all day'. The union between the two wild children is interrupted when Cathy stays with the Lintons. What effect do you think the stay will have on Cathy and, as a result, Heathcliff? Try and make some predictions, comparing your ideas with other students in a small group.

4 With Frances's arrival, update the Earnshaw family tree you started in Chapter Four (see page 143).

5 The two houses (Wuthering Heights and Thrushcross Grange) and those who live in them represent several contrasts. In Chapter Five we see two: the interiors and the children. Read pages 44 and 45 again. For a description of Wuthering Heights, go back to pages 8 and 9. In which of the two houses do we find or expect to find these things? Complete the table.

1 ferocious dogs indoors
2 elegant, comfortable furniture
3 legs of meat hanging from the ceiling
4 white stone floors
5 two clean, well-dressed children
6 a tidy, well-looked after garden

Wuthering Heights	Thrushcross Grange
4	

6 Now fill in the equivalent for the other house.

CAE 7 Work in pairs. Student A should describe Wuthering Heights. Student B should describe Thrushcross Grange. Contrast the two houses and their inhabitants.

Cathy stayed at Thrushcross Grange for five weeks, till Christmas. By that time her ankle was healed [1] and her manners were much improved. When she came home, I expected a wild little savage without a hat to rush in and hug [2] us all so tightly we couldn't breathe; but, instead of that, a very dignified, handsome, well-dressed young lady appeared on a black pony.

'Cathy, what a beauty you are!' cried Hindley. 'You look like a lady now.'

'She must be careful not to grow wild again now that she is home,' said Frances.

Cathy kissed me very lightly indeed, because I was covered in flour from making the Christmas cake, and she did not want to get her clothes dirty. Then she looked around for Heathcliff.

'Heathcliff!' called Hindley. 'Come forward and greet Miss Catherine, like the other servants.'

Heathcliff came forward slowly. He looked even dirtier and wilder than he had done before she left. She ran up to him and kissed him seven or eight times. Then she looked at him and laughed. 'How very black and angry you look!' she said. 'And funny and grim! That's because I'm used to looking at Edgar and Isabella Linton. Well, Heathcliff, have you forgotten me?'

Shame and pride had made him gloomy and unresponsive. [3]

---

1. **healed** : healthy again.
2. **hug** : embrace tightly and warmly.
3. **unresponsive** : silent.

'Go on, Heathcliff,' said Hindley condescendingly. [1] 'You are allowed to shake her hand.'

'I will not!' cried Heathcliff at last. 'I will not be laughed at!'

'I did not mean to laugh at you, Heathcliff,' said Cathy. 'It was only that you looked strange. If you wash your face and brush your hair, you will be all right. But you are so dirty!'

'I like to be dirty!' cried Heathcliff, and he left the room. Hindley and Frances were very amused by this scene, but Cathy was deeply disturbed by it. She did not know what she had said to upset him so.

Hindley and Frances took Cathy off to the drawing room to show her the presents they had bought for the young Lintons. Edgar and Isabella had been invited to Wuthering Heights the following morning, and their mother had agreed that they could come, on condition they were 'kept away from that gypsy boy'.

I went into the kitchen and looked around with pleasure and pride at all my preparations for Christmas: the shining silver, the clean floor, the fragrant cakes. I remembered how the old master used to come into the kitchen on Christmas Eve and thank me for my work and give me a shilling [2] as a Christmas present. Then I began thinking about how fond the old master was of Heathcliff, and how worried he was that Heathcliff would be treated badly when he was no longer there to take care of him. Then I thought about poor Heathcliff's situation now, and it nearly made me cry. However, there is no use in crying, so I went to find Heathcliff instead.

He was feeding the horses in the stable, as usual at that hour. 'Come quickly, Heathcliff,' I said. 'Come to the kitchen and let me

---

1. **condescendingly** : with superiority.
2. **shilling** : unit of money used in Britain until 1971.

dress you nicely before Miss Cathy comes out. Then you can sit together by the fire and talk till bedtime.'

He went on feeding the horses in silence.

'Are you coming?' I waited and waited, but, receiving no answer, I finally left him.

Cathy ate supper with her brother and sister-in-law, while Joseph and I ate together in the kitchen. Heathcliff did not eat at all. He worked till nine o'clock then went straight to bed. Cathy came into the kitchen to look for him once, but, since he was not there, she went back to Hindley and Frances.

Heathcliff got up early in the morning and went out onto the moors. He came back when the family had gone to church. 'Nelly,' he said, 'dress me nicely as you said you would. I'm going to be good.'

'At last!' I said. 'You have hurt Cathy, you know. I bet she's sorry she came home. It looks as if you envy her for being so elegant and having friends.'

The idea of envying Catherine was incomprehensible to him, but the idea of hurting her was clear enough. 'What makes you think I hurt her, Nelly?'

'She cried when I told her that you had gone off to the moors this morning.'

'Well, I cried last night, and I have more reason to cry than she.'

'Yes,' said I. 'You had the reason of going to bed with a proud heart and an empty stomach. If you are sorry now, you must say so to Cathy. Kiss her and say you are sorry. Come, now. I'll wash you and dress you so nicely that Edgar Linton will look like a doll beside you. You are younger than he is, but you are taller and broader in the shoulders and stronger too.'

Heathcliff looked happy for a moment, then he frowned [1] again. 'But, Nelly, he is much more handsome than I am. I wish I had light hair and fair skin and fine clothes and the prospect of being rich, as he does!'

'Come to the mirror, and I'll show you what to wish,' I said, when I had finished washing and dressing him. 'You should wish that your frown would go away and that your eyes would look out on the world boldly and confidently, instead of suspiciously, as they do now.'

'I should wish for Edgar Linton's great blue eyes and smooth forehead, Nelly. But that won't help me get them.'

'A good heart will help you to a handsome face,' I said. 'But look at yourself now. Now we've finished with the washing and dressing, don't you think you are rather handsome? I do! You look like a prince in disguise. Perhaps your father was Emperor of China and your mother an Indian queen. If I were you, Heathcliff, I would believe something of the sort, and it would give me the courage and the dignity to endure the oppressions of a little farmer like Hindley Earnshaw!'

So I chattered [2] on, and gradually Heathcliff stopped frowning and began to smile. Then we heard the Lintons' carriage arriving, and behind them the Earnshaws on their horses (they always went to church on horseback). Catherine brought Edgar and Isabella into the sitting room and sat them down by the fire, which soon put a little colour into their white faces. I told Heathcliff to hurry into the sitting room and present himself, and he willingly obeyed. Unfortunately, as he entered the sitting room, he met Hindley, who pushed him back towards the kitchen, crying, 'Joseph! Keep Heathcliff out of the sitting room.'

1. **frowned** [fraʊnd] : looked in a disapproving way.
2. **chattered** : talked.

'Oh, sir,' I said. 'Let him stay. He'll be good.'

'Go away, you vagabond! Look at this! How clean and elegant you are! I'll pull your hair until it is even longer!'

'It's long enough already,' said Edgar Linton. 'It looks like a horse's mane.'[1]

Edgar did not mean to be insulting, but Heathcliff could not bear this remark from someone he already considered a rival. He picked up a bowl of hot apple sauce and threw it over Edgar, who immediately burst into tears. Catherine and Isabella ran over to Edgar's side. Hindley grabbed[2] Heathcliff and took him to his room, where I have no doubt he hit him, because when Hindley returned his face was red and his breathing heavy.

I got a towel and scrubbed[3] Edgar's face quite hard, telling him that he should not have interfered. Isabella started weeping and saying that she wanted to go home. Cathy stood there, blushing for everyone.

Hindley tried to cheer everyone up. 'Come, come,' he said. 'There is a delicious lunch waiting for us. Let's forget about this unfortunate incident and enjoy ourselves.'

They all sat down, and I served the food. I was surprised and disappointed to see Catherine eat her goose with a good appetite and no signs of distress. She is an insensitive child, I thought to myself. How easily she forgets Heathcliff's troubles. But just then her eyes filled with tears. She dropped her fork on the floor deliberately, so that she could hide her face under the table until the tears were gone.

When I tried to take Heathcliff a plate of food, I discovered

1. **mane** : long hair on the back of its neck.
2. **grabbed** : took hold of forcefully.
3. **scrubbed** : cleaned vigorously.

that he had been locked in his room. After lunch some musicians came from the village, and there was singing and dancing. Cathy asked if Heathcliff could come downstairs now, but Hindley said no. Later on, Cathy said she wanted to listen to the music from the top of the stairs. I thought she would go up to the attic, where Heathcliff's room was, to talk to him through the locked door. When the music was about to end, I went upstairs to warn her. She was not outside Heathcliff's door, but I could hear her voice within. The little monkey had climbed out of the window, along the ledge, [1] and in through the window of Heathcliff's room. When she came out again, Heathcliff came with her. She insisted that I take him to the kitchen. I did not like to deceive my master, but since Heathcliff had not eaten all day I agreed.

Heathcliff was quiet and thoughtful. When I asked him what he was thinking about, he said, 'I'm trying to decide how to pay Hindley back. I don't care how long I wait. I just hope I do not die before I do it.'

'For shame, Heathcliff!' said I. 'It is for God to punish wicked people; we should learn to forgive.'

'No,' said Heathcliff. 'God won't enjoy it as much as I will. Leave me alone to make my plans, Nelly: while I'm thinking of that, I don't feel pain.'

But, Mr Lockwood, you must be tired. I have been chattering on too long, giving too many details. I could have told you Mr Heathcliff's story in half an hour.

Thus interrupting herself, Mrs Dean stood up and began to put her sewing away.

'Oh, Mrs Dean, please stay!' I cried. 'Do stay another half

---

1. **ledge** : narrow protruding step on the exterior of the house.

hour. You did right to tell the story slowly. That is the method I like, and you must finish in the same style.'

'But it's eleven o'clock, sir.'

'Never mind. I will sleep late tomorrow morning.'

'Oh, you shouldn't do that, sir. You miss the best part of the day.'

'But I think I have a cold, Mrs Dean, and will probably stay in bed all day tomorrow. So please sit down again and go on with your story. I am fascinated by your characters. They seem to live much more earnestly than city people do. City people are too concerned with surface change and frivolous external things. But here a life-long love seems almost possible. I have always thought it impossible for love to last more than one year.'

'When you get to know us,' said Mrs Dean, 'we country people are like people everywhere else.'

'No, Mrs Dean,' I replied. 'I don't believe it. You, my good friend, are a striking example of what I mean. You have thought much more than most servants think, and I believe that is because you have lived all your life here: you have been forced to reflect upon things, because here you have no frivolous entertainments on which to waste your time.'

Mrs Dean laughed.

'I certainly think of myself as a sensible woman,' she said. 'Not because I live in the country, but because my life has been disciplined, and also because I have read more than you think, Mr Lockwood. There is not a book in the library that I have not looked into and learned something from, except of course those in Latin and Greek and French.'

Well, I will continue my story like a true gossip, but I will pass on to the following summer — which was the summer of 1778 — nearly twenty-three years ago.

Go back to the text

1 Catherine's return to Wuthering Heights was a surprise. Imagine Mrs Dean meets a friend in the village and they talk about Catherine. How does Mrs Dean reply to these questions? Complete the table below.

Mrs Dean's friend	Mrs Dean's reply
I suppose she was as badly dressed as ever; no shoes, or hat!	
Did she run into the kitchen and hug you all?	
Quite the little lady! I imagine she ignored Heathcliff.	

CAE **2** For questions 1-5, choose the appropriate answer (A, B, C or D).

1 How did Cathy feel at having offended Heathcliff?

A ☐ satisfied

B ☐ confused

C ☐ angry

D ☐ amused

2 What was Heathcliff's immediate response to Mrs Dean's suggestion to get washed and changed?

A ☐ He refused.

B ☐ He told her to leave him alone.

C ☐ He ignored her.

D ☐ He accepted it.

3 Heathcliff could not understand the idea of

A ☐ envying Catherine.

B ☐ hurting Catherine.

C ☐ leaving Catherine.

D ☐ loving Catherine.

4 Heathcliff wanted to

    A ☐ look like Edgar Linton.

    B ☐ be rich like Edgar Linton.

    C ☐ speak like Edgar Linton.

    D ☐ dress like Edgar Linton.

5 Heathcliff threw apple sauce over Edgar

    A ☐ because Edgar had deliberately insulted him

    B ☐ because Heathcliff was angry at being different from the others

    C ☐ to provoke Hindley

    D ☐ to annoy Cathy.

3 **Mrs Dean's humanity and intelligence characterise the chapter. Lockwood himself remarks on this at the end of the chapter. Find examples.**

4 **Which of the following statements regarding Catherine do you agree with? Compare your answers with other students. Give reasons why.**

    1 Catherine is essentially a socially conventional character.

    2 Catherine is divided in equal measure between her need for social convention on one hand and a wildness of spirit on the other.

    3 Catherine's wild personality is only in part held back by her contact with conventional society outside Wuthering Heights.

5 **At the end of Chapter Four Mrs Dean hinted at Heathcliff's vindictive nature. How is this confirmed in Chapter Six?**

On the morning of a fine June day, the last of the ancient Earnshaw family was born, and I was his nurse. His mother died in childbirth. She had been ill with tuberculosis for a long time. But he was the finest, healthiest, handsomest baby I had ever seen. I took care of the child as if he were my own. No one interfered with me. Hindley was satisfied just to see that he was healthy. He had never had any love in his heart for anyone except himself and his wife. Now that she was gone, he spent his time drinking and cursing. He was so offensive that soon all the other servants left, except for Joseph and me. I did not want to leave the baby, and Joseph was always content to be where there was plenty of evil to reprove.

Hindley's treatment of Heathcliff was enough to turn a saint into a devil, and I believe that there was something diabolical about Heathcliff at that time. He enjoyed watching Hindley degrade himself. The house was like hell. The curate stopped coming to visit. Nobody decent came near Wuthering Heights, except Edgar Linton, who came to visit Cathy. At fifteen years old, she was the queen of the countryside, the most beautiful girl around, but she had become proud and bad-tempered. I admit I did not like her at that time. She still liked me, though. She was always loyal to her old friends, and young Linton, despite his superiority, found it difficult to make an equally deep impression on her.

'Do you see that portrait over the fireplace? That was Edgar

Linton, my late master. It used to hang on one side and his wife's portrait hung on the other side, but hers has been removed.'

Mrs Dean raised her candle and went to the fireplace. The delicate features of Edgar Linton's portrait were very much like those of the young lady at Wuthering Heights, but his expression was gentle and thoughtful, very different from hers. His light hair was long and curly; his eyes were large and serious; his figure was almost too graceful. I was not surprised that Catherine Earnshaw could forget her first friend for a man like this. More surprising was that he — if his mind were as noble and delicate as his person — could fall in love with the kind of woman I imagined her to be. Mrs Dean sat down and began her story again.

Catherine continued her friendship with the Lintons, and began to live a double life. She did not show her wild side to them: she was polite and friendly to Mr and Mrs Linton; she won the admiration of Isabella and the heart and soul of Edgar. This pleased her well, for she was very ambitious.

At Thrushcross Grange, where she had heard Heathcliff described as a 'vulgar ruffian' and 'worse than an animal', she was careful not to act like him; but at home she did not bother to be polite or to restrain [1] her wild nature.

Mr Edgar did not dare come to Wuthering Heights often. He was afraid of Hindley's drunken rages. Catherine was not sorry: she did not like to see her two friends together. If, when Linton was absent, Heathcliff expressed contempt for him, Catherine could seem to agree. Similarly, if Linton showed disgust for Heathcliff in Heathcliff's absence, she could pretend to be

---

1. **restrain** : control.

indifferent. She could use neither of these tricks when both were present.

One day Hindley was away, so Heathcliff decided to take the day off work. He asked Cathy to spend the day with him, but she said she was expecting Edgar Linton. Heathcliff went off on his own, feeling angry, hurt, and jealous.

When Edgar Linton arrived, Cathy told me to leave the room. I was polishing [1] the silver. 'You can go now, Nelly,' she said, in that imperious way of hers.

Now the master had told me to stay with them whenever Edgar Linton came to visit, so I replied, 'I'll just finish polishing this silver, Miss Cathy. I'm sure Mr Linton does not mind.'

She came up to me, and, supposing that Edgar could not see her, she pinched my arm. It really hurt a lot, and I was determined that Mr Linton should notice it. 'Oh, miss!' I cried. 'Why did you pinch me?'

'I didn't touch you, you lying creature!' said Catherine, and she tried to pinch me again, her face red with rage.

'Yes, you did, miss. Here!' and I showed the purple mark on my arm, so that Mr Linton could see it.

She slapped my face so hard that my eyes filled with water.

'Catherine, love! Catherine!' cried Linton, shocked by her behaviour.

'Leave the room, Ellen!' said Catherine, trembling all over.

Little Hareton, who followed me everywhere, was in the room, and when he saw her slap me he began to cry. Now she grabbed his shoulders and shook him violently. Edgar tried to

---

1. **polishing** : cleaning.

free the child from her grasp, [1] so she slapped him across the cheek as well! I took little Hareton and went off to the kitchen, but I left the door open so that I could see what happened. Edgar turned pale and picked up his hat. I thought, That's right! You've seen her true character now! Take warning and go!

'Where are you going?' asked Catherine. 'You must not go!'

'I must and shall!' said Edgar.

Catherine dropped onto her knees by a chair and burst into tears.

Edgar left the sitting room, but once outside the front door he hesitated. I called encouragement to him from the kitchen window: 'You had better go home, sir! Miss has a very bad temper indeed!'

He turned abruptly and ran back into the sitting room. When I went in later, to tell them that Hindley was coming home drunk, I saw that the quarrel had only served to make them closer. It was clear that they were no longer merely friends: they were lovers.

1. **grasp** : (here) hands.

Go back to the text

1 Which two events open and close Chapter Seven?

2 'The house was hell.' A recurring theme throughout *Wuthering Heights* is evil. How do the following inhabitants of Wuthering Heights create this situation?

1 Hindley : ....

2 Heathcliff : ....

3 Joseph : ....

3 Complete the table illustrating Catherine's double life.

At Thrushcross Grange	At Wuthering Heights
she was polite to Mr and Mrs Linton	she had no interest in being polite she did not defend Edgar from Heathcliff's abuse

4 What do the events in this chapter tell you about Edgar's personality and his feelings towards Cathy?

CAE 5 Imagine you are Mrs Dean. Write a letter (approximately 250 words) to a friend, describing what you know about Cathy's 'true character'.

6 In Chapter Eight, Hindley comes home drunk. What do you expect him to do? Choose one of the following. Compare your ideas with a partner, giving reasons for your choice. Then read Chapter Eight, and see if you were right.

1 He attacks Catherine.

2 He attacks Edgar Linton.

3 He attacks his son, little Hareton.

4 He attacks Heathcliff.

5 He attacks Mrs Dean.

Edgar had left by the time Hindley came in, drunk and swearing at the top of his voice. I put Hareton in the kitchen cupboard to keep him safe from his father. The poor little thing remained perfectly quiet wherever I chose to put him.

'Where's my son!' shouted Hindley, grabbing me by the back of the neck, as if I were a dog. 'I'll kill you, Nelly, if you don't tell me where he is! I'll stick this carving knife down your throat!'

'I don't like the carving knife, Mr Hindley,' said I. 'I have been cutting fish with it, and it smells. I'd prefer to be shot, please.'

'You'd prefer to be damned! Open your mouth.' He pushed the point of the knife between my teeth. I spat it out and said it tasted awful. Just then I saw Hareton standing at the door, crying pitifully.

Hindley saw him too, dropped the knife and grabbed the child, who only cried all the louder. 'What's wrong with him? Doesn't he love his father? What an unnatural child!' cried Hindley, but the child kept screaming. Hindley ran upstairs and held little Hareton over the banister. [1] 'Be quiet and kiss your father, or I'll drop you!' cried Hindley. I rushed up to save the child, but as I reached the top I saw Hindley bend forward over the banister. 'Who is that coming in?' he asked vaguely, and Hareton wriggled [2] out of his grasp and fell. There was hardly time to feel a thrill of horror when we saw that the child was safe. Heathcliff, whose step we had heard, arrived below and instinctively caught the child in his arms.

---

1. **banister** : posts and rail fixed on the sides of a staircase.
2. **wriggled** : made small quick movements, turning from side to side.

But when he looked up and saw that it was Hindley who had let Hareton drop, his face showed clearly that he regretted having caught the child. His vengeful heart would have enjoyed watching the drunken father weep for the son he had accidentally killed.

Hindley came downstairs and poured himself a glass of brandy. 'Oh, sir, you've had more than enough already!' I cried, trying to take the glass from his hand. 'Have mercy on this unfortunate child, if you have none on your own soul!'

He raised the glass out of my reach and made a toast,[1] 'Here's to my own soul's damnation!' cried the blasphemer. 'Now get out of my sight, all of you!'

I went to the kitchen to comfort little Hareton. Heathcliff walked through the kitchen. I thought he had gone out to the stables to feed the horses, but later I discovered that he had lain down on a bench by the wall, far away from the light of the fire, and remained silent.

I rocked Hareton in my arms and sang a song to him that began,

'It was late at night and the babies cried,
And their mother heard them in her grave...'[2]

Then Miss Cathy, who had heard all the trouble from her room, came in and whispered, 'Are you alone, Nelly?'

'Yes, miss,' I replied.

She came up beside me, and I saw a tear roll down her cheek. For a moment I thought she had come to say she was sorry for having treated me so badly. But no, she was upset about her own concerns, as usual. 'I'm so unhappy!' she said.

---

1. **toast** : normally an expression of good wishes or respect.
2. **grave** : tomb.

'What a pity,' said I. 'You have everything in the world, and yet you can't be happy!'

'Today Edgar Linton asked me to marry him, Nelly, and I gave him an answer. Before I tell you what my answer was, I want you to tell me what it should have been.'

'Really, Miss Cathy, I don't know. If he asked you after your dreadful behaviour, you probably should have refused him, because he must be a fool.'

'I accepted him, Nelly. Be quick! Say whether I was right or wrong!'

I put Miss Cathy through a sort of catechism.

'Do you love him?' I asked.

'Yes, I do.'

'Why do you love him?'

'Because he is handsome and pleasant.'

'Bad!' said I.

'And he loves me.'

'That's a little better, but not much.'

'And he will be rich, and I would love to be rich!'

'Worst of all! Now, tell me why you are unhappy. Your brother will be pleased that you are to marry Mr Linton, and his parents will not object. You will escape from a disorderly comfortless home to a wealthy respectable one. You love Edgar, and he loves you. All seems smooth and easy — where is the obstacle?'

'Here and here!' cried Catherine, striking her forehead and then her breast. 'Wherever the soul lives — in my soul, in my heart, I am convinced that I am wrong!'

'I don't understand you,' said I.

She was silent for a while, then she said, 'Nelly, do you ever have strange dreams?'

'Sometimes.'

'So do I. I've dreamt dreams that have stayed with me ever after and changed my ideas. They've gone through me, like wine through water, and changed the colour of my mind. And this is one. I'm going to tell it, but you must not smile at any part of it.'

'Very well,' said I.

'I dreamt I was in heaven, Nelly, but I was extremely miserable. Heaven did not seem to be my home, and I wept and wept until the angels became angry and threw me out, and I landed in the middle of the moors at Wuthering Heights, and I woke up sobbing for joy. That will explain my secret. I should not marry Edgar Linton any more than I should live in heaven. And if Hindley had not brought Heathcliff so low, I would never have thought of it. It would degrade me to marry Heathcliff now, so he shall never know how I love him.'

I noticed a movement in the shadows, and saw that Heathcliff had been there, listening, all the time. He crept out silently. Cathy did not notice anything. She went on, 'I don't love Heathcliff because he's handsome; I love him because he's more myself than I am. Whatever our souls are made of, his and mine are the same, and Linton's is as different as moonbeam from lightning or frost from fire. My great miseries in this world have been Heathcliff's miseries. If all else perished [1] and he remained, I would go on living; but if he perished, the universe would seem a great stranger to me, and I would not seem to be a part of it. My love for Linton is like the leaves on the trees: time will change it, I know. My love for Heathcliff is like the eternal rocks

---

1. **perished** : died.

beneath: a source of little visual delight, but necessary. Nelly, I am Heathcliff — he is always in my mind — not as a pleasure, any more than I am always a pleasure to myself — but as my own being.'

'But think, Miss Cathy, if Heathcliff loves you as you say you love him, how terrible it will be for him to lose you.'

'Lose me? Why should he lose me? We shall be together as we always have been. But you see, Nelly, if I married Heathcliff, we would have no money. If I marry Edgar, I can help Heathcliff to rise and place him out of my brother's power.'

'Well, Miss Cathy, that is the worst reason you have given so far for marrying Edgar Linton. I can't understand your nonsense, miss, and I must make the dinner, so tell me no more secrets, please.'

When dinner was ready, I went to look for Heathcliff, but I could not find him. By this time there was a great thunderstorm, and wind and rain were lashing [1] the moors. I told Cathy that Heathcliff had heard part of what she had said to me, and now he was nowhere to be found. She cried out, as if in pain, and ran to find him herself. She ran to the top of the hill and called out his name. Then she sent Joseph out to search for him on the moor, and I went to look for him in the barn, but none of us found him. We did not see Heathcliff again that night or for years to come.

At this point Mrs Dean looked at the clock. 'My goodness, Mr Lockwood, it's midnight! I must be off and let you sleep!' And indeed I did want to sleep. I felt weak and ill, with aching head and limbs.

1. **lashing** : hitting.

Go back to the text

1 The chapter can be divided into two main parts: Hindley's drunken rage and Catherine's confiding in Mrs Dean. Answer the following questions for each part.

1 **Hindley's drunken rage**

A Several shocking things happen on Hindley's return. What are they? Discuss with a partner which you think is the worst.

2 **Catherine confides in Mrs Dean**

A Why does Cathy decide to marry Edgar?

B '(Dreams have) gone through me, like wine through water, and changed the colour of my mind.' Read Cathy's conversation with Mrs Dean carefully. She uses several vivid similes (a phrase which compares one thing to something else, using the words 'as' or 'like'). Complete the table with the words in the list below she associates with Edgar and Heathcliff.

fire   leaves   lightning   moonbeam   rock

Edgar	Heathcliff

2 How do these similes help us to understand the nature of her relationships with Edgar and Heathcliff?

3 In Cathy's dream she is thrown out of heaven and returns 'sobbing for joy' to Wuthering Heights. On the basis of the recurring image of Wuthering Heights and its inhabitants presented in the story, what is your interpretation of her dream? Discuss your ideas in small groups.

4 Heathcliff disappeared and was not seen again 'for years to come'. How do you imagine Cathy's immediate future without him? Make a list of your ideas. Think about the following points.

1   Where she will live

2   Her lifestyle

3   Her personality

CAE **5** Read the text below and decide which word best fits each space. The exercise begins with an example (0).

Heathcliff (**0**) ...C..... part of Catherine's confession to Mrs Dean and realises that Catherine (**1**) .... to marry Edgar Linton. (**2**) .... , Heathcliff leaves Wuthering Heights. At this stage of the story there are two thematic contrasts: one is represented by Wuthering Heights and Thrushcross Grange, (**3**) .... the other by the two loves in Catherine's life, Heathcliff and Edgar. Brontë uses this (**4**) .... of putting two elements together (**5**) .... compare and contrast them to (**6**) .... It is not easy to decide (**7**) .... the writer wants the reader to take one (**8**) .... rather than the other. Should we condemn Catherine or (**9**) .... her? Should we respect the Lintons or detest them? The continuing fascination of the story probably lies in the role readers have (**10**) .... having to answer these questions for themselves.

0	**A** overlooks	**B** oversees	**C** overhears	**D** overstates
1	**A** intends	**B** will	**C** decides	**D** knows
2	**A** Naturally	**B** Hopefully	**C** Consequently	**D** Ideally
3	**A** while	**B** when	**C** but	**D** though
4	**A** trick	**B** tool	**C** device	**D** mode
5	**A** to	**B** for	**C** so	**D** thereby
6	**A** themselves	**B** the other	**C** others	**D** each other
7	**A** why	**B** when	**C** what	**D** whether
8	**A** hand	**B** side	**C** aspect	**D** argument
9	**A** criticise	**B** object to	**C** attack	**D** idealise
10	**A** on	**B** in	**C** for	**D** at

I was very ill for four weeks. The first day that I was strong enough to see anybody, Mr Heathcliff came with gifts of meat and wine. He sat by my bedside for an hour and talked to me. I wanted to say to him, 'Scoundrel! [1] This is all your fault! If I had not passed that terrible night at your house, I would never have got ill like this!' But I said nothing: I was grateful for his company.

I am feeling much better today. I think I will ask Mrs Dean to come and sit by my bedside and finish her tale.

Mrs Dean came.

'Please continue with your story, Mrs Dean,' said I. 'Miss Cathy was engaged to Edgar Linton. Heathcliff had run away. What happened then?'

Mrs Dean brought out her sewing and continued her narrative.

That night, Miss Catherine spent many hours walking in the rain on the moors, looking for Heathcliff. She never found him, and when she came home she was shivering [2] with fever. When Mr and Mrs Linton heard of her illness, they very kindly invited her to stay with them until she was healthy again. Unfortunately both Mr and Mrs Linton caught the fever from her, and both died shortly afterwards.

Miss Catherine married Edgar Linton, and she and I moved to Thrushcross Grange. To my surprise, she behaved well there. She seemed to love Mr Linton almost too much and was very affectionate to his sister. They did all they could to make her

1. **scoundrel** : person with no moral conscience or principles.
2. **shivering** : shaking slightly from the cold.

happy. I noticed that Mr Linton was very much afraid of her anger. He talked to me once, when I had given a sharp answer to one of her imperious orders. 'Nelly, for my sake, [1] do not anger her. Nothing hurts me so much as to see her displeased.'

So, for my kind master's sake, I was gentle with my mistress, and for six months the gunpowder lay harmless, because no fire came near to ignite it. Sometimes Catherine was gloomy and sad. Then her husband took great care of her and sympathised with her. He thought these fits of sadness were a result of her illness: she had never been subject to depression of spirits before. When she felt better and smiled again, so did he. But their happiness did not last long.

One mild evening in September, I was coming in from the garden with a heavy basket of apples. It was dusk, and the moon was rising, causing shadows to lurk in the corners. I put the basket down on the step by the kitchen door, and sat down beside it to rest and breathe the soft sweet air.

'Nelly, is that you?' whispered a deep voice from the darkness.

Then, in the shadows, I saw a tall man in dark clothes with dark skin and hair. I did not recognise him at first, but when he stepped forward into the light, I saw his eyes. I recognised his eyes.

'Are they at home, Nelly?' he asked. 'Where is she? I must speak with her. Go and tell her a person from the village wants to speak to her.'

'How will she take it?' I exclaimed, 'What will she do? The surprise will drive her mad. You are Heathcliff, but different — changed. What have you been doing all these years?'

'Go and give her my message. I'm in hell until you do!'

---

1. **for my sake** : in order to help me.

I went into the drawing room, where Mr and Mrs Linton were sitting so peacefully. I felt reluctant to deliver the message. After lighting the candles, I muttered, 'There is a person from the village who wishes to see you, madam.'

When she had left the room, Mr Edgar asked me who it was, and I told him. 'What?' said he. 'The gypsy? The plough-boy?'

'You should not call him by those names, master,' I said. 'She would be hurt if she heard you.'

He opened the window and called down, 'Bring the person in, my dear.'

In a few moments, Cathy ran into the room, her face flushed [1] with excitement. Heathcliff followed her in. Now that I saw him properly in the light, the change was even more apparent than before. He had grown into a tall strong man; my master looked a slender youth beside him. The way Heathcliff stood and walked — so straight and proud — suggested that he had been in the army. His face looked intelligent and refined — there was no sign of his former degradation — but there was something ferocious about it still; the eyes were still full of black fire.

My master's surprise equalled or exceeded my own. He stood confused for a moment, unsure how to address the 'plough-boy', as he had called him. 'Sit down, sir,' he said, after a while.

Heathcliff sat opposite Catherine. She never took her eyes off him. It was as if she were afraid that he might vanish again if she did. He did not look at her often — a quick glance now and then — but each time his glance drank delight from hers and he looked more confidently. They were too absorbed in their own pleasure to think of anyone else. Edgar watched them with a pale face. At

---

1. **flushed** : coloured.

one point, Cathy jumped up and grasped Heathcliff's hands, laughing. 'I shall think it was a dream tomorrow!' she said. 'I can't believe I have seen, touched, and spoken to you once more. And yet, cruel Heathcliff, you don't deserve this welcome! You stayed away three years and never thought of me!'

'I heard of your marriage, Cathy, and so I thought I would come back one more time. I would have a glimpse [1] of your face — you would look surprised and pretend to look pleased. Then I would go and kill Hindley. I would get my revenge at last. And then I would kill myself before the law did so. That was my plan. But now that you have welcomed me so warmly, I have changed my mind. I'll not go away again. I've had a hard life since you last saw me, and I struggled only for you!'

'Come, come, the tea is getting cold,' said Edgar, trying to speak in his normal voice.

Miss Isabella came in, and Catherine poured out the tea.

I don't know what was said at the meal, because I withdrew [2] to the kitchen. An hour later, Heathcliff left. 'Are you staying in the village?' I asked him at the door.

'No,' he said. 'I am staying at Wuthering Heights. Mr Earnshaw invited me when I called upon him this morning.'

I was very surprised to hear this and began to think that it would have been better for everyone had Heathcliff stayed away.

1. **glimpse** : quick look.
2. **withdrew** : moved away.

Go back to the text

1 Put these events from Chapter Nine into their correct order.

A ☐ Catherine marries Edgar Linton.

B ☐ Heathcliff returns.

C ☐ Catherine catches a fever while looking for Heathcliff.

D ☐ The Lintons invite Catherine to Thrushcross Grange.

2 Until Heathcliff reappears Catherine manages to keep the dark side of her personality under control. Mrs Dean says she was like 'gunpowder (that) lay harmless, because no fire came near to ignite it'.

1 What occasional signs are there of her dark side?

2 What 'ignites' Cathy's dark side?

3 Catherine marries Edgar Linton. Update the family tree (see page 143).

3 Before Mrs Dean tells the Lintons of Heathcliff's arrival, she says 'I went into the drawing room, where Mr and Mrs Linton were sitting so peacefully.' Why do you think Mrs Dean adds this last piece of information?

4 Heathcliff has changed but in what ways is he still the same?

CAE **5** Heathcliff is on his way back to the north of England. You are sitting next to him on the stage coach.

Student A: You are Heathcliff. Answer student B's questions about your plans. You are not particularly friendly, and you do not speak very much.

Student B: You are Heathcliff's travelling companion. You are interested by this tall strong man with dark eyes. Find out as much as you can about his plans. Start the conversation, and encourage Heathcliff to speak more.

Student B: What are you going to do when you arrive in the village?

Hindley invited Heathcliff to remain at Wuthering Heights permanently as his tenant. Heathcliff now had plenty of money, and he would pay a good rent. Hindley needed money, because he drank and gambled away [1] all he had. Heathcliff, apparently, lent money to Hindley to pay off his gambling debts. I learned all this from late-night conversations with Catherine. She loved to talk about Heathcliff, and if she talked about him to Edgar, Edgar looked hurt and sad.

Heathcliff was a frequent visitor at Thrushcross Grange. Mr Linton did not like these visits, but he tolerated them for his wife's sake. After a while, however, it became apparent that Miss Isabella was infatuated with Heathcliff. She became bad tempered and moody, pale and thin. One day she lost her temper with Cathy.

'You are harsh and unkind to me, Cathy!' she cried.

'Don't be silly, Isabella. When have I ever been harsh or unkind to you?'

'Yesterday! In our walk on the moor. You told me to walk off on my own, because you wanted Heathcliff all to yourself.'

'Nonsense! I thought our conversation might bore you, that was all.'

'I didn't care about the conversation. I just wanted to be close to — '

'Well!' said Catherine, suddenly understanding.

---

1. **gambled away** : lost by playing games of chance for money.

'You are always sending me away. You want no one to be loved except yourself! I love him more than you ever loved Edgar, and he might love me, if you would let him!'

'I wouldn't be you for a kingdom, then,' declared Catherine emphatically — and she seemed to speak sincerely. 'Nelly, help me to convince her of her madness. Tell her what Heathcliff is — a savage creature. You only think you love him because you do not know him. Please don't imagine that he has a loving heart beneath that stern exterior. He is a fierce, pitiless, wolfish man. He could not love a Linton, but he might marry you for your money. Then, if you irritated him, he would crush you like a sparrow's egg, Isabella.'

'You just say so because you want him for yourself!' cried Isabella.

'Very well. I have warned you,' said Catherine coldly, and she left the room.

'She was lying, wasn't she, Nelly?' sobbed Isabella. 'He must have a noble heart, or how could he have loved her for so long? He is not a devil, but a faithful loving man.'

'Forget him, miss,' said I. 'Mrs Linton spoke harshly, but I cannot contradict her, and she knows him better than I do. Honest people don't keep secrets. How has he been living? How has he got rich? Why is he staying at Wuthering Heights, the house of a man he hates? I saw Joseph the other day, and he told me that Mr Earnshaw has got worse since Heathcliff arrived. They sit up all night together, drinking and gambling. Hindley has borrowed a lot of money from Heathcliff, offering the house and land as security. Joseph says that Hindley is galloping down the road to hell, and Heathcliff is running before him, opening all the gates. Do you want such a man for a husband, miss?'

'You are on Catherine's side!' cried the infatuated girl. 'You are just saying these things to keep me from being happy!'

The next day, Heathcliff came to visit. Catherine and Isabella were sitting in silence together when he arrived. 'Ah!' cried Catherine when he came in, 'Heathcliff, here, at last, is someone who loves you more than I do! No — don't look at Nelly — it's not her; it's my poor little sister-in-law, who is breaking her heart over you. If you wish, you can be Edgar's brother! No, no, Isabella, you shan't run off. We were quarrelling like cats about you, Heathcliff, and Isabella tells me that, if I would stand aside, she would shoot an arrow of love into your heart that would make you forget me forever!'

'Let me go, Catherine!' cried Isabella in distress. 'Mr Heathcliff, please do not listen to her. She is joking, but I find her joke painful in the extreme.'

'Heathcliff, doesn't my news make you happy?' continued Catherine, holding Isabella's arm tightly. 'Why, Isabella has not eaten for two days because she is so angry with me for having sent her away when we were walking on the moors. She says I wanted to deprive her of your company.'

'Well,' said Heathcliff, looking at Isabella as one might look at a strange repulsive animal, a centipede from India, for example. 'She clearly does not want to be in my company now.'

Poor Isabella went pale then blushed red. She tried to prize [1] Catherine's fingers from her arm but could not, so she scratched them.

'Ah! What a tigress! Go away, for God's sake! How foolish you

---

1. **prize** : force to separate.

were to show him your tiger-claws! Look, Heathcliff,' said Catherine, showing him the crescents of red on her hands. 'You must be careful she doesn't scratch your eyes out with them!'

'I'd tear them off her fingers, if they ever menaced me,' he answered brutally, when the door had closed behind Isabella. 'But you were not speaking the truth, were you?'

'Indeed I was,' said Catherine.

'How strange. If I lived alone with that pale insipid face, I would turn those blue eyes black before long, and paint her face the colours of the rainbow.' He fell silent and looked thoughtful for a while, and then he said, 'She is her brother's heir, is she not?'

'Not for long. Soon I will have sons to be my husband's heirs. You covet [1] your neighbour's goods too much, Heathcliff! Remember this neighbour's goods are mine.'

From that day onwards, I watched Heathcliff closely. My heart was with my master's interests, more than with Catherine's. He was kind, trustful, and honourable; and she — she could not be called the opposite, yet she seemed to allow herself such wide latitude. I had little faith in her principles and less sympathy for her feelings. I wished that Heathcliff would go away again. His visits to the Grange were a continual nightmare to me, and, I suspected, to my master too. I hated to think of Heathcliff living at Wuthering Heights. I felt that Hindley was like a stray [2] sheep, forsaken [3] by his good shepherd, and Heathcliff was like an evil beast, prowling [4] close by, awaiting the right moment to spring and destroy.

1. **covet** : desire what belongs to someone else.
2. **stray** : lost.
3. **forsaken** : abandoned.
4. **prowling** : moving quietly as if hunting.

Go back to the text

1 At the end of Chapter Nine Mrs Dean says, 'it would have been better for everyone had Heathcliff stayed away'. Summarise the dramatic effects his presence has on:

1   Hindley   2   Isabella

2 Catherine warns Isabella about Heathcliff. How does Heathcliff's behaviour in this chapter confirm Catherine's warning?

3 Linton and Heathcliff are completely different. Even their love for Catherine differs. The differences are developed by vocabulary. Look at the vocabulary associated with Edgar in this chapter. Complete the table with vocabulary showing Heathcliff's violent nature.

Edgar	Heathcliff
he looked hurt and sad	
he tolerated (Heathcliff's visits)	
he (Edgar) was kind, trustful, and honourable	

4 Heathcliff wants Thrushcross Grange. What do you think he will do to get it?

CAE **5** Discuss your ideas in groups, then write a report of approximately 250 words summarising your conclusions.

The next day, I was standing by the window when Heathcliff arrived. Isabella was in the courtyard below. When he saw her, he went up to her and talked to her in an earnest agitated way. Then he grabbed hold of her and kissed her. I cried out, and Catherine came over to see what was the matter.

She called Heathcliff in, and locked herself in the kitchen with him. There they had a terrible argument. I could hear bits of it as I passed by. Heathcliff told her that she had treated him infernally. He insulted my master, and he swore he would have his revenge. My master, meeting me on the stairs, asked where Mrs Linton was. I told him she was shut up in the kitchen with Heathcliff, and I told him what had happened in the courtyard. He was furious. He called two of the gardeners to help him and went to the kitchen. There he demanded that Heathcliff leave his house and never return again. Heathcliff called him a coward and might have hit him, but Catherine said, 'Go now, Heathcliff,' and he obeyed her.

After Heathcliff had gone, Catherine and Edgar argued. I heard some of what was said. My master at one point said that Catherine had to choose between Heathcliff and himself. Soon after that, she went to her room and locked herself in. All that day and the next she stayed in her room and refused to eat the meals I brought her. I thought she was pretending, trying to make Edgar feel sorry that he had argued with her. Edgar sat in his study, gloomy and depressed, with books open before him, but he was not reading. Isabella wandered round the courtyard, weeping most of the time. I went about my normal household duties, convinced that there was only one sensible soul at Thrushcross Grange, and that was lodged [1] in my body.

On the third day, Catherine asked for some water and food. She said she was dying. I was still sure it was all an act. I brought her some tea and toast, and she ate it hungrily. 'Where is Edgar, Nelly? What is he doing?' she asked.

'He is reading in his study, madam,' said I.

'Reading? Reading? Doesn't he know that I am dying? Haven't you told him, Nelly?'

'No, I haven't.'

'Then go and tell him now! Tell him that I am starving myself. Tell him how pale and thin I look.'

'I shall tell him you just ate some toast and drank some tea, and you seemed to enjoy them.'

1. **lodged** : fixed.

'If I were sure it would kill him, I would kill myself right now!' she said suddenly. 'These three awful nights, I have not slept at all. I have been tormented, Nelly. But now I see that you don't like me. How strange! I thought that everyone loved me, even though they hated and despised each other. But now I see that they are all my enemies. How sad to die surrounded by enemies! Open the window, Nelly, and let me breathe the fresh air. Let me breathe the air from the moors!'

'It's cold, madam. You should stay warm in bed and try to sleep.'

'If you won't open it, I will,' she cried, and, before I could stop her, she opened the window wide and leaned out into the icy wind. I begged her to close the window and get back into bed. I tried to pull her away from the window, but she was delirious — I knew that now — and it gave her a strength far greater than mine.

'Last night, Nelly, I thought I was lying in my old oak case bed at Wuthering Heights. The tree was tapping on the window, and I was crying because Hindley had separated me from Heathcliff. I lay alone for the first time, crying my heart out. Then I put my hand out, expecting to touch the window sill, but I touched the table instead, and I knew that I was here at Thrushcross Grange. Oh, Nelly, I wish I were a girl again, half savage and brave and free... Why have I changed so much? I'm sure I would be myself again if I could walk on the moor. Open the window!'

Just then my master came in.

'Oh, sir,' said I. 'My poor mistress is ill. Please come and help me to keep her in her bed.'

'Catherine ill? Why was I not told?' he asked, shocked at the sight of her thin pale face.

'She would not let anyone into her room until this evening, sir, so I didn't know myself how ill she was, but it is nothing.'

'It is nothing, is it, Ellen Dean?' said my master sternly. He took his wife in his arms and looked at her with anguish. 'It is all your fault. You told me about Heathcliff. You caused our argument.'

'I was just doing my duty as a faithful servant,' said I.

I left the house to go to the village and find the doctor. On my way out, I saw Miss Isabella's little dog hanging by a rope from a tree in the garden. The poor dog was nearly dead when I cut the rope and released it. I wondered who could have done such a thing and why, but I had no time to think about that. I ran to the village as fast as I could.

When the doctor heard that Catherine Linton was ill, he came back to the Grange with me immediately. 'Has her illness anything to do with this business of Mr Heathcliff and Miss Isabella?' he asked, much to my surprise.

'Why, doctor! How do you know about that?'

'Well, they were seen riding by a few hours ago. Some people in the village saw Mr Heathcliff riding by and Miss Isabella on the horse behind him.'

'Good Lord!' I cried. When we got to the house, I ran to Isabella's room, but she was gone. What could I do? I could not pursue them. And I could not tell my master about it. The poor man was absorbed in the calamity of his wife's illness. How could I tell him of a second calamity now? I decided to say nothing. The next morning, however, one of the servants came back from the village and told him everything. At first he could not believe it, but when we showed him Isabella's empty room, he said, 'She had a right to go if she wanted to. Trouble me no more about her.'

Go back to the text

1 These are the main events in the chapter. Fill in those that are missing.

1   Heathcliff kisses Isabella.

2   ....

3   Heathcliff is ordered by Edgar to leave Thrushcross Grange.

4   ....

5   Catherine falls ill.

6   Edgar is angry at Mrs Dean for not having been told about his wife's condition.

7   Mrs Dean goes to call the doctor.

8   ....

9   The doctor tells Mrs Dean that Heathcliff and Isabella were seen together.

10 A servant tells Mr Linton the news of his sister's disappearance.

2 Mrs Dean says, 'I was convinced that there was only one sensible soul at Thrushcross Grange, and that was lodged in my body.' What is the condition of the other inhabitants?

1   Edgar   2   Isabella   3   Catherine

3 Dreams play an important role in *Wuthering Heights*. What do you think Cathy's dream means? Work in a small group and try and interpret her dream. Compare your interpretation with other groups.

4 What are your reactions to what happened to Isabella's dog? Who do you think did this to the dog?

CAE 5 On hearing of Isabella's decision to go to Wuthering Heights, Edgar says 'trouble me no more about her'. Why? Which of these statements do you agree with? Discuss your ideas with a partner. Can you suggest any other reasons?

1   He feels that Isabella has disgraced the Linton family and he can no longer forgive her.

2 He is unable to cope psychologically with the suffering which Heathcliff has caused.

3 He cannot understand Isabella's behaviour, which goes completely against his own personality.

4 He is secretly pleased with his sister's decision as it puts a greater distance between Catherine and Heathcliff.

'I wish I were a girl again…'

Catherine expresses a regret about her present situation. We can express present regrets using the form *'I wish'* or *'if only'* + **past simple**.

We can also have regrets about the past. We can express past regrets using the form *'I wish'* or *'If only'* + **past perfect**.

6 Rewrite these characters' present regrets using 'I wish' or 'If only'.

1 **Edgar**: My poor wife can't free herself of her obsession for Heathcliff.

2 **Mrs Dean**: I'm the only sensible person at Thrushcross Grange.

3 **Isabella**: Why doesn't Heathcliff love me like I love him?

7 Now rewrite these characters' regrets about the past using 'I wish' or 'If only'.

1 **Hindley**: Why did my father bring Heathcliff to Wuthering Heights?

2 **Catherine**: I didn't want Heathcliff to hear my conversation with Nelly

3 **Edgar Linton**: Why did Heathcliff ever decide to return to Wuthering Heights?

8 Now think of some other regret that any of the characters might have made during the course of the novel. Say when they would have expressed this regret.

CHAPTER 12

Two months passed. Mr Edgar took constant care of Catherine, and gradually she began to get better. This was a double blessing, because, we now discovered, she was expecting a baby.

Isabella had sent a short note to Edgar, saying that she was married to Heathcliff. The note seemed cold and unfeeling, but beneath the signature some more was scribbled [1] in pencil. She was sorry, she said, to have caused her brother pain. She hoped that he remembered her kindly and that they could be reconciled. Linton did not reply to the note. Two weeks later, I received a letter from her. I have the letter here. I'll read it to you:

'Dear Ellen,

'I arrived at Wuthering Heights last night. Since Edgar did not reply to my note, I am writing to you. Please tell him that I would give anything to see his face again. My heart turned to Thrushcross Grange twenty-four hours after I had left it. I miss my old home so much! And I miss Edgar and Catherine. I cannot come to see them, even though I want to more than anything.

'Ellen, tell me, how did you keep from going mad when you lived here at Wuthering Heights? The people here all seem inhuman. And, tell me, is Mr Heathcliff a man? If so, is he mad? And, if not, is he a devil? I will not tell you the reasons I ask these questions, but please answer them. Please explain, if you can, what I have married. Come and see me, Ellen, very soon. Don't disappoint me.

Isabella.'

1. **scribbled** : written quickly and untidily.

I told my master about the letter. He said I should go to Wuthering Heights, but that he could not see Isabella or write to her. I set out the next day and walked to Wuthering Heights. The house was sadly changed since my time there. The pewter dishes and silver tankards in the sitting room were covered with dust. Isabella looked lost and rather bedraggled. [1] Hindley seemed on the verge of madness. Hareton was like a little animal. Only Heathcliff looked well: only he had the look of a born gentleman.

'Tell me about Catherine,' said Heathcliff. 'I hear she has been ill.'

'Mrs Linton is just recovering,' said I. 'She will never be as she was, but at least she is alive. Her appearance and her character have both changed greatly. Mr Linton will stay by her, for he is her husband, but now his affection can only be the result of remembering what she once was, of common humanity and a sense of duty.'

'That is quite possible,' said Heathcliff, trying to keep calm. 'It is possible that your master might feel nothing for Catherine but common humanity and a sense of duty. But I will not abandon her to his duty and humanity. Promise me that you will help me to see her. I will see her anyway, with or without your help.'

'Mr Heathcliff, you mustn't see her, and you never will with my help. Another argument between you and my master would kill her.'

'If you help me, I can see her without his knowledge,' he said. 'If he died, would Catherine suffer greatly from his loss? The fear that she would is the only thing that stops me from killing him. I would never do anything to hurt her.'

'And yet,' said I, 'you are planning to go and see her now,

---

1. **bedraggled** : untidy.

when she has nearly forgotten you, even though that might make her ill again!'

'You think she has nearly forgotten me?' he said. 'Oh, Nelly! You know she has not! You know as well as I do that she thinks of me much more than she thinks of Linton. If I believed that she had forgotten me, my life would be hell.'

'Catherine and Edgar love each other!' cried Isabella, suddenly furious. 'You have no right to talk like that!'

'What do you know about love?' said Heathcliff scornfully. 'You thought you loved me, and you were fool enough to think I might love you! But you know nothing about it. For you, I was a kind of hero of romance. You must have been mad to think so! And, Nelly, how hard it was to persuade her to hate me! I hanged her little dog before we left the Grange, and I said I wished I could hang everyone in that house except for one. She, like a fool, thought I meant her. And, thinking herself safe, she did not find my brutality disgusting. But I have managed it at last. This morning she told me that she hates me. She can leave me if she wants to. I used to enjoy tormenting her, but now she simply bores and irritates me.'

'Mr Heathcliff,' said I, 'this is the talk of a madman. Since you now say that she can leave, I am sure she will.'

'He says I can leave,' cried Isabella with glittering [1] eyes, 'but he said that before, and I tried to leave, and I dare not try again! He has told me that he married me solely to gain power over Edgar. But I won't let him gain power over Edgar! I'll die first! Nelly, you must promise not to repeat this conversation to Edgar or Catherine.'

1. **glittering** : producing small, bright flashes of light.

'Enough!' cried Heathcliff. 'Go to your room. I want to talk to Ellen alone.'

When Isabella had left the room, Heathcliff said, 'Last night I was in the Grange garden for six hours, Nelly, and I'll return there tonight and every night until I find an opportunity of entering. If I meet Edgar Linton, I will knock him down. If he sends his servants to throw me out, I will threaten them with these pistols. Wouldn't it be better, Nelly, to prevent my coming in contact with your master or his servants?'

'I won't do it, Mr Heathcliff! My mistress is nervous and anxious. The shock of seeing you would be too much for her. It would kill her, I'm sure. Give up this plan, for her sake! If you won't, I will tell my master, and he will make sure that you never get in the house!'

'You won't get home tonight to tell him, Ellen Dean!' cried Heathcliff. 'I'll keep you here until I have seen her. You say the shock of seeing me will kill her. I don't want to shock her. You will ask her if I may come. You think she has forgotten me because she never speaks of me, but how can she speak of me when everyone in the house is a spy for her husband? It must be like hell for her in that house! You say she is nervous and anxious. How the devil could it be otherwise, in her terrible isolation? With that weak insipid creature watching over her out of a sense of duty and humanity! He might as well plant an oak tree in a flower pot and expect it to grow! How can she regain her health in the shallow soil of his love? You must decide now, Nelly! Will you stay here, while I go to the Grange and fight my way into her room? Or will you be my friend, as you have been in the past?'

Well, Mr Lockwood, I argued and refused to help him fifty times, but in the end he won. I agreed to carry a letter to my mistress. If she agreed to see Heathcliff, I would inform him of Linton's next absence from the house. Then he would come to see her. Was it right or wrong? I fear it was wrong. At the time I hoped to prevent another explosion. The doctor is coming to see you now, Mr Lockwood. I'll finish my story another time.

So saying, Mrs Dean left the room. And what a dismal story it is! But never mind. Perhaps I can extract good medicine from Mrs Dean's bitter herbs. Perhaps it will teach me to be careful of the fascination of Catherine Heathcliff's brilliant eyes. What if I fell in love with her, and she turned out to be a second edition of her mother!

Go back to the text

1 In Chapter Ten, Isabella ignores Catherine's warnings about Heathcliff. In this chapter, how is Catherine proved right?

2 An atmosphere of decay, evil and madness dominates Wuthering Heights. What does Mrs Dean find when she goes to visit Isabella?

3 Heathcliff ridicules Edgar's love for Catherine when he says 'he might as well plant an oak tree in a flower pot'. Which of these statements about Heathcliff do you agree with? Compare your views with other students.

1 Heathcliff is convinced of the superiority of his love for Catherine.

2 He is jealous of Edgar's love for Catherine.

3 He fears Catherine may love Edgar more than him.

4 He knows Catherine loves him more deeply than Edgar.

5 He despises the feelings of people like the Lintons.

6 He accepts the inevitability of Catherine's marriage to Edgar Linton.

4 Catherine is expecting a child. Lockwood met this child as an adult at the beginning of the story. Who do you think it was?

CAE 5 Mrs Dean finally agrees to take Heathcliff's letter to Catherine. Imagine you are Heathcliff and write the letter to Catherine (approximately 250 words).

6 How do you think Catherine will react to the letter?

Extension Activities – Part 1

1 **Summarise the main events of Part 1 in a list. For example:**

1 Lockwood goes to Wuthering Heights and meets its inhabitants.
2 Lockwood is forced to spend a night at Wuthering Heights.
3 He has a nightmare.
4 Mrs Dean begins telling Lockwood her story.

Compare your events with other students in a small group. Decide on the most important. Using them, write a short summary.

2 A **'Several characters, their backgrounds and their actions, remain mysterious.' In Part 1 what mysteries are there regarding Heathcliff, Hindley and Frances?**

B **What effects do these mysteries have?**

CAE **3** **'Heathcliff: monster or victim?'**
Divide your class into two groups: A and B.

Group A will support the proposition 'Heathcliff is a monster'.
Group B will defend Heathcliff, supporting the proposition that 'Heathcliff is a victim'.

Keep a note of your views and use evidence from the book to support your ideas ('For example, if we look at Chapter Nine we can see…'). Now work in pairs, one student from group A and one from group B. Discuss your views.

4 **After you have finished, write a brief summary of your discussion. Use some of the following phrases.**

'My partner, defending the proposition…, started by pointing out that… . He/she went on to say that… . However, I thought that…'

The Imaginative World
of the Brontë Children

The Reverend Patrick Brontë and his wife, Maria Branwell Brontë, had six children: Maria, Elizabeth, Charlotte, Branwell, Emily and Anne. They lived at the parsonage in Haworth, a small village on the Yorkshire moors. When, in 1821, Mrs Brontë died of cancer, her sister, Elizabeth Branwell, came to live at the parsonage and take care of the children, who were still very young. Maria – the eldest – was eight years old when her mother died, and the youngest – Anne – was still a baby. Elizabeth Branwell was a very religious woman, with stern Calvinistic views. Her warnings of eternal punishment made a deep impression on her young nieces and nephew. Joseph's grim religious pronouncements in *Wuthering Heights* were probably based on Emily's memories of her Aunt Elizabeth.

In 1824 Maria, Elizabeth, Charlotte and Emily were sent to the Cowan Bridge School for clergymen's daughters. Charlotte's description of Lowood School in *Jane Eyre* draws upon her experience of the harsh conditions at Cowan Bridge. Maria and Elizabeth died of tuberculosis in 1825, as a result of those conditions: cold, damp and a poor diet. The Reverend Brontë withdrew Charlotte and Emily from the school and took them home, where he and their aunt supervised the rest of the girls' education.

That year, Tabitha Ackroyd came to Haworth parsonage as a domestic servant. She remained in the household for thirty years and was a strong influence upon the young Brontës. Tabitha – known in the family as 'Tabby' – had a wide knowledge of folk tales and superstitions. She was rather strict with the children, but she was also very fond of them, and in the evenings she told them stories –

local legends in which the familiar setting of the Yorkshire moors was the scene of magical events and ghostly apparitions. These, like Aunt Elizabeth's tales of hell and damnation, had a profound effect on the children's imaginative development.

One day in June 1826 – when Charlotte was ten years old, Branwell was nine, Emily was eight, and Anne was six – the Reverend Brontë gave them a dozen wooden soldiers. They played with the soldiers and began inventing stories about them. At first, the stories were set in an imaginary city in Africa called Glass Town. Later, entire countries emerged: the kingdoms of Angria and Gondal. Charlotte and Branwell recorded the saga of Angria in a series of tiny notebooks. Emily and Anne, meanwhile, recorded the Gondal saga. Full of magic, drama, violence and romance, the sagas show the influence of the children's favourite books: *Aesop's Fables*, *The Arabian Nights*, Gothic novels and Romantic poetry. Gondal and Angria became a secret world, unknown to the adults in the household. In this world of the imagination, anything could happen, and the Brontë children could escape the isolation and strict routine of Haworth parsonage.

We are used to thinking that, in the Victorian period, women were less likely to succeed professionally than men, because of the restraints placed upon them by a patriarchal society. However, of the four children who created that imaginary world, only the son, Branwell, failed to realise his early promise. He lived a short, unhappy life, became an alcoholic, and died at the age of thirty-one. All the surviving daughters, Charlotte, Emily and Anne, wrote poetry and novels that are now considered classics. Of all the works they produced in adult life, Emily's *Wuthering Heights* is the one that most fully reflects the imaginative influences of their shared childhood.

Haworth parsonage seen from the churchyard.

CAE ① Write a leaflet on Haworth parsonage and the surrounding area for visitors (approximately 250 words). Use the Internet to help you find out more information (for instructions, see page 116).

Part 2

CHAPTER **13**

Another week has passed, and I am nearly well again. I have now heard all my neighbour's story, and will write the rest down here in Mrs Dean's words.

The following Sunday, when my master was at church, I brought Heathcliff's letter to my mistress. All the windows and doors of the house were open to let in the mild spring air, and she was sitting by her bedroom window, wearing a loose white dress.

'There is a letter for you, madam,' I said, and I placed it in her hand. She did not look at it or respond at all. After a while, I said, 'It needs an answer. It is from Mr Heathcliff.'

She started and looked at the letter with hungry eager eyes, but clearly she did not understand what it said. 'He asks if he may come and see you,' I said. She sighed and leaned back in her chair but did not respond. It was clear to me that my poor mistress would never be well again.

Just then I heard Heathcliff's step on the stairs. The open house had been too much of a temptation for him. She heard it too, and stared at the door with glittering eyes. Then he was by her side and had grasped her in his arms. He did not speak or let go of her for five minutes; he just held her tightly and kissed her over and over again. His face was buried in her hair, and it struck me that he probably could not bear to look at her face, so clear were the signs there that she was sure to die.

'Oh, Cathy! Oh, my life! How can I bear it!' he cried in despair.

'What now?' said Catherine, leaning back to look at his face. 'You and Edgar have broken my heart, Heathcliff! And you both come to me and cry as if you were the people to be pitied. I shall not pity you! You have killed me, and it has done you good. How strong you are! How many years do you plan to live after I am dead?'

Heathcliff had knelt on one knee to embrace her. Now he tried to rise, but she grabbed his hair and kept him down.

'I wish I could hold you until we were both dead,' she said bitterly. 'Will you forget me and be happy when I am in the earth? Will you say, "That is the grave of Catherine Earnshaw. I loved her long ago, but I have loved others since, and I love my children more than I ever loved her." Will you say so, Heathcliff?'

'Don't torture me till I'm as mad as you are!' cried Heathcliff, tearing his head free from her grasp so violently that some of his hair was left in her hand. 'You must be possessed by a devil to talk to me that way, when you are dying. Don't you realise that every word will be burnt into my memory? I will think about these words of yours again and again forever after you are gone.' He left her side and walked over to the fireplace. There he stood with his back to her, so that she could not see his face.

'Heathcliff, don't be angry now,' said Catherine, rising from her chair. 'Do come to me, Heathcliff!' He turned to her, his eyes wet with tears, then Catherine leapt towards him, and they were locked in an embrace from which I thought my mistress would never be released alive. It seemed to me that she had fainted in his arms, and I went closer to see if she was all right. Heathcliff glared [1] at me, breathing heavily like a mad dog. He did not seem like one of my own species. Then Catherine put her arm around his neck and her cheek against his.

'Why did you betray your own heart, Cathy?' he cried. 'You loved me! What right had you to leave me? You say I have killed you, but you killed yourself. You say I broke your heart, but you broke your own heart by marrying Linton, and you broke mine too. Do you think I want to live? I wish I were not strong and healthy. What kind of life will it be when you — oh, God! Would you like to live with your soul in the grave?'

Just then I saw the servants and my master returning from church. 'You must go, Mr Heathcliff!' I cried. 'He will be here in a minute!'

'Catherine, I must go,' said Heathcliff, trying to extricate himself from her embrace.

'No! You must not go!' she replied, holding him tightly. 'Don't go! This is the last time! I shall die!'

Heathcliff sat down again and stroked her hair, whispering, 'Hush, [2] my darling. I'll stay. Don't worry.' But she was limp [3] in his arms, and her eyes were shut. I thought she had either fainted or died. It would be better, I thought, if she had died.

I heard my master coming up the stairs. There was cold sweat on my forehead: I was horrified. When he saw Heathcliff, Edgar went white with rage, but Heathcliff stood and said, 'Take care of her first. You can talk to me later,' and he left the house.

At midnight that night the Catherine you saw at Wuthering

1. **glared** : looked angrily.
2. **hush** : relax, be quiet.
3. **limp** : not stiff or firm.

Heights was born. Two hours later, her mother died. Linton's grief was too painful to describe. I believe it was made even worse by the fact that he had no heir. Old Mr Linton had left Thrushcross Grange to his own daughter, Isabella, if Edgar should have no sons. Now Edgar's daughter would be left with nothing.

As the sun rose, my master lay on Catherine's pillow, exhausted by grief, his living face as pale as the dead face beside him. I went outside into the park, where I was sure I would find Heathcliff waiting. I found him standing under a tree. He must have been standing still for a very long time, because two birds were hopping [1] on the ground beside him, as if he were a piece of wood. When I approached, they flew away.

'I know she's dead,' said Heathcliff. 'How did she die, Nelly?'

'Very peacefully. She did not speak again after you left. She died very early this morning. She looks so peaceful now. Let's hope she may wake to peace in the other world!'

'May she wake in torment!' cried Heathcliff with sudden passion. 'Catherine Earnshaw, may you not rest, as long as I am living! You said I killed you — haunt me then! The murdered do haunt their murderers, I believe! Be with me always — take any form — drive me mad! Just don't leave me here alone without you! Oh, God! I cannot live without my life! I cannot live without my soul!'

He dashed [2] his head against the tree trunk until his forehead was stained [3] with blood; he howled and sobbed, not like a man but like a savage beast in torment.

---

1. **hopping** : jumping.
2. **dashed** : hit.
3. **stained** : (here) covered.

Go back to the text

CAE **1** **For questions 1-7, choose the correct answer (A, B, C or D).**

1 Mrs Dean explains the contents of Heathcliff's letter to Catherine because

   A ☐ Catherine is too scared to read it.

   B ☐ Catherine is too weak to read it.

   C ☐ Catherine seems not to understand.

   D ☐ Catherine refuses to read it.

2 As soon as Heathcliff sees Catherine he

   A ☐ embraces her.

   B ☐ tells her how unhappy he is.

   C ☐ stands in silence.

   D ☐ starts crying.

3 At first, how does Catherine speak to Heathcliff?

   A ☐ softly

   B ☐ lovingly

   C ☐ disinterestedly

   D ☐ angrily

4 Heathcliff embraces Catherine a second time after

   A ☐ she moves towards him.

   B ☐ he moves towards her.

   C ☐ Mrs Dean moves closer to Catherine.

   D ☐ Mrs Dean leaves the room.

5 When Edgar returns

   A ☐ Heathcliff refuses to leave.

   B ☐ Mrs Dean asks him to stay.

   C ☐ Heathcliff leaves immediately.

   D ☐ Catherine asks him to stay.

6 Catherine Earnshaw dies

A ☐ in childbirth.

B ☐ shortly after childbirth.

C ☐ a long time after childbirth.

D ☐ and her child dies too.

7 Edgar's child would have been left Thrushcross Grange if

A ☐ she had been a boy.

B ☐ Edgar hadn't married Catherine.

C ☐ Isabella had not married Heathcliff.

D ☐ Isabella had not had any children.

2 Heathcliff and Catherine are one of literature's great tragic couples. Find some examples of language that conveys their passionate feelings.

3 Catherine is Heathcliff's obsession both in life and death. What evidence have we seen so far of Catherine's haunting him till he dies?

4 Review the Earnshaw/Linton family tree (see page 143). Test your partner with some questions such as 'Who is Hindley?'

5 Think back to the beginning of the story. Put the names of the main characters into the correct circle below (WH = Wuthering Heights, TG = Thrushcross Grange).

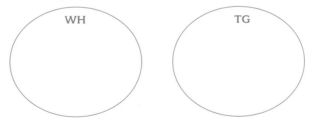

6 At the end of Part 1, Wuthering Heights and Thrushcross Grange are no longer separate worlds. Now where would you put the characters? How have these changes taken place?

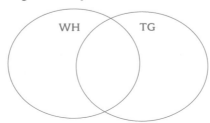

CHAPTER 14

One week later, I was in the sitting room with Catherine's baby girl. It was a stormy evening: the wind blew and the rain changed gradually to snow. My master was asleep upstairs. He had spent most of the week up there with his sorrow. Suddenly the door opened, and Isabella ran in, soaking wet and laughing like a mad woman. There was a bleeding cut below her ear. She wore no coat or hat, and her dress was wet with rain and snow.

'Nelly!' she cried. 'I have run away! I have left that monster! Call me a carriage, so that I can go to the village. I dare not stay here! As soon as he knows that I am gone he will come here after me.'

'Miss Isabella, I will call no carriage until you have calmed down and changed into dry clothes. What on earth has happened?'

'All week, Heathcliff has stayed away from the house, returning late at night and shutting himself in his room. Hindley has been drinking more and more. He has a gun and a knife, and he told me he was going to kill Heathcliff. He says that Heathcliff has robbed him and Hareton and me too, that he has stolen all we have. He says that Heathcliff now owns Wuthering Heights: he lent Hindley so much money for gambling and drink that now the house belongs to him. Yet I could not stand by and watch Hindley shoot him. When Heathcliff returned, I opened the window and warned him that Hindley had weapons and would kill him. Heathcliff forced his way into the house and tore the weapons from Hindley's hands, wounding him with the knife as he did so. I rushed to Hindley to nurse his bleeding hand, and I said to Heathcliff, "Oh why did you come back to the house? Why don't you just lie down on Catherine's grave like a faithful dog?" Heathcliff threw the knife at me, and it cut me just below the ear. I turned and left the room. Heathcliff probably thinks I went to my own room and locked myself in, but instead I ran from the house, and I swear I will never sleep another night at Wuthering Heights!'

I gave her dry clothes and a coat and hat. I made hot tea for her and called a carriage. Within an hour she left for the village and the next morning she moved on towards London. She never came back to this neighbourhood again, but she wrote letters to her brother regularly. From these we learned that she had given birth to a son a few months after she left Wuthering Heights. She said he was a sickly, peevish [1] child, always ill, always crying. She christened him Linton Heathcliff.

Someone told Heathcliff about the child, and, when I met him by chance in the village, he asked me what name they had given him. When I told him, he smiled bitterly and asked if they wanted him to hate the child too. 'But I will have him when I want him, they can be sure of that!'

My master lived a very quiet life after Catherine's death. He hardly ever left Thrushcross Grange now. Gradually his grief subsided. [2] He was sure that Catherine was in heaven, and he remembered her with tender love. His affectionate nature turned to his little daughter, who was christened Catherine in memory of her mother.

---

1. **peevish** : easily annoyed by unimportant things.
2. **subsided** : became less intense.

Six months after Catherine died, Hindley died too. He got very drunk and locked himself in his room. The next morning, Heathcliff and Joseph heard him moaning. [1] Heathcliff sent Joseph to get the doctor, but by the time they returned Hindley was dead. Joseph was very upset. He told me he wished he had stayed and let Heathcliff go for the doctor. 'I should have stayed with the master,' Joseph said. 'If he was going to die, he should have died with a faithful servant by him. But he wasn't dead when I left — far from it!'

After the funeral, Heathcliff said to Hareton, 'Now you are mine! And I'll be as kind to you as your father was to me!'

'That boy should go back to Thrushcross Grange with me,' I said.

'Does Linton say so?' asked Heathcliff, frowning.

'Yes. He told me to bring the boy home.'

'But I want the boy to stay with me,' said Heathcliff. 'And if Linton takes him, I will want my own son to come and take his place.'

That stopped any plans to bring Hareton to Thrushcross Grange. There was nothing we could do for him. The family lawyer told Edgar that Hareton was left a beggar: his father had died penniless, and his only chance in life was to gain Heathcliff's affection. So Hareton was now completely dependent upon his father's enemy. Heathcliff treated him like a servant, though he paid him no wages. [2] The guest was now the master at Wuthering Heights.

---

1. **moaning** : making a low sound expressing pain.
2. **wages** : salary.

Go back to the text

1 How has Isabella been damaged by her contact with Wuthering Heights?

2 Birth and death

1 **Birth**: Linton Heathcliff: What is significant about his name?
2 **Death**: How does Hindley die? What does Joseph think about the circumstances of his master's death?

3 'Hareton becomes Heathcliff and Heathcliff becomes Hindley'. Can you explain this sentence? What do you think Hareton's life at Wuthering Heights will be like after the death of his father?

4 Hareton could not go to Thrushcross Grange for two reasons. What were they?

5 Update the Earnshaw/Linton family tree (see page 143).

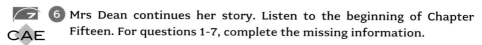

6 Mrs Dean continues her story. Listen to the beginning of Chapter Fifteen. For questions 1-7, complete the missing information.

CAE

1 After a period of sadness came a period of ....
2 This period lasted .... years and coincided with Catherine's ....
3 In appearance, Catherine was like her mother: she had .... eyes; and like her father: her .... was pale and her hair was ....
4 Like her mother, she was lively and ....
5 Probably like her father, her anger was never .... and her .... never fierce.
6 Catherine's world in those years was exclusively ....
7 Her father didn't let her .... and didn't want her to ....

7 Which title for the extract you have heard do you prefer and why? Discuss your ideas with other readers.

1 The calm before the storm
2 Happiness at last
3 Her mother's daughter
4 Trapped

The twelve years that followed that dismal period were the happiest in my life. I took care of young Catherine and watched her grow. She was such a little beauty that she seemed to bring sunshine into the house. Her eyes were dark like her mother's but her skin was pale and her hair was yellow and curling like the Lintons'. She was lively but not rough, a very affectionate child, as her mother had been, but not really like her mother. Young Catherine could be soft and mild as a dove. She had a gentle voice and a pensive expression. Her anger was never furious, her love never fierce.

For the first twelve years of her life, she lived at Thrushcross Grange, hardly ever leaving the grounds. [1] She knew nothing of Heathcliff and Wuthering Heights. Sometimes she looked at the hills beyond the park and asked me what they were like and whether I had been there. She wanted very much to go beyond the gates of the park and wander on those hills with her little horse. However, her father did not want her to know about Heathcliff and Wuthering Heights. He told her she could go when she was older.

That year, Isabella fell ill. She wrote to Edgar and asked him to come to her. She said that she was going to die, and she wished to arrange everything for her son Linton. She asked Edgar to take her son to live with us at Thrushcross Grange after she was dead. Edgar went to see her as soon as he received this letter. He told me to take good care of Catherine while he was gone and to make sure she did not leave the grounds of Thrushcross Grange. He was gone for three weeks.

1. **grounds** : land or gardens that surround a building.

At first, Catherine played in the house, but then she got bored and asked if she could ride around the park on her pony. I let her go, and for several days she enjoyed herself wandering around the extensive grounds of Thrushcross Grange. One day, however, she was not back by tea time. I sent the servants to look for her, but she was nowhere to be found. In panic, I went to look for her myself. Clearly she had left the park. I remembered her questions about the hills and felt sure she had gone there, so I walked out of the park, across the moor, and up the hill as quickly as I could. When I came to Wuthering Heights, I saw a woman in the yard. She was the housekeeper. 'Hello,' she said. 'Are you looking for the little girl? Don't worry. She's safe in our sitting room.'

'Is she with Mr Heathcliff?' I asked.

'Oh no,' said she. 'Mr Heathcliff and Joseph are away. They won't be back until late. Come in.' I followed her into the sitting room, and there, by the fire, was Catherine, sitting in her mother's old chair, talking to Hareton. They looked up when I came in, and I noticed that they both had the first Catherine's dark eyes.

'Come on, Miss Cathy, we're going home,' I said.

'Oh, not yet, Nelly. I want to stay here a little longer,' replied Cathy.

'If you knew whose house this was, you would be glad to leave,' I said.

'It's your father's house, isn't it?' said Cathy, turning to Hareton.

He blushed red and did not reply. 'Or is it your master's house? I see now! You are a servant! Well, then, you should get my horse, and I will go home. You should have told me you were a servant.'

'Damn you![1] I'm not a servant!' cried Hareton furiously.

'What? Nelly! Did you hear what he said to me? How dare he?'

'Well, miss,' said the housekeeper. 'You shouldn't tell him what to do. He is not a servant: he is your cousin.'

'My cousin?' exclaimed Cathy, staring at his long hair and

---

1. **damn you** : expression of anger.

dirty clothes. 'He can't be! My father has gone to get my cousin and bring him home to live with us.'

'You have more than one cousin,' I said, hurrying her out of the house. On the way home, I explained to her about Wuthering Heights. I told her that her father did not want her to know about it, and, if he discovered that she had been there, he would be very angry with me. Cathy promised to say nothing to her father on the subject. After all, she was a sweet little girl.

The next day, we received a letter saying that my master was coming home. Isabella was dead, and Edgar was bringing her son Linton home to live with us. Catherine was very excited. When the carriage arrived, she ran to meet it, eager to see her cousin, but her father stopped her and said, 'Now, Cathy, you must be very gentle and patient with Linton. He is not well, and he is very sad because his mother has just died. He won't be able to play with you yet.'

Linton was carried into the house. He looked very much like Edgar — the same fair curly hair, slim figure, delicate features, and pale skin — but his expression was sickly and peevish, not at all like the open, honest, affectionate expression of Edgar's face. At first, Cathy sat by him, still and silent, but then she began to stroke his hair and kiss his cheek. He seemed to like this treatment and smiled at her weakly.

That night, when the children were asleep, Joseph came to speak to my master. 'Heathcliff has sent me to get his son,' said Joseph.

Edgar was silent for a minute. He wanted to obey Isabella's last wish and keep the boy at Thrushcross Grange, but Heathcliff was the boy's father. 'Tell Mr Heathcliff that his son shall come to Wuthering Heights tomorrow,' said Edgar. 'He is asleep in bed now. He is not in good health. And tell him that the boy's mother wished him to live here with me.'

'Heathcliff doesn't care about what the mother wished!' said Joseph. 'He wants the boy, and he wants him now!'

'Not tonight!' said Edgar. He took the old man by the arm and led him to the door.

As the door closed behind him, Joseph cried out, 'Heathcliff will come himself tomorrow! You won't dare to throw him out!'

Early the next morning, my master told me to take the boy to Wuthering Heights. Cathy was still in bed when we left. On the way, Linton asked me many questions about his father: 'Why did my mother never tell me about him? Why did he not live with us, as other fathers do? Why did he never come to see us?' I answered these questions as briefly as possible, trying to calm the boy.

When we got to Wuthering Heights, Heathcliff, Joseph, and Hareton came out to greet us. They all stared at Linton with curiosity. 'Good Lord!' said Heathcliff. 'Look at him! He is certainly his mother's son: there's none of me in him! Look how pale and thin and sickly he is! But never mind. He is mine. And he is the heir of Thrushcross Grange. It will give me great satisfaction to see my son the master of that house! You need not worry about him, Nelly. I will take good care of him. I wouldn't want him to die before he is master of Thrushcross Grange. I have hired a tutor for him, and I have told Hareton to obey him. I will raise him as a fine gentleman. It is a pity that he is such a weak miserable creature, but he will be master even so!'

As I rode back alone to Thrushcross Grange, I felt sorry for the boy, but at least, I thought, Heathcliff's selfishness will make him treat the boy well.

Go back to the text

1 The chapter can be divided into two parts: before and after Linton Heathcliff's arrival at Thrushcross Grange. Where does the second part begin?

2 In Part 1, Catherine makes two mistakes about Hareton's identity. What are they? Correct them.

	Mistake	Correction
1		
2		

3 Catherine Linton and Linton Heathcliff are cousins. What are the physical similarities and differences between the two? Complete the table with appropriate adjectives from the chapter.

SIMILARITIES	DIFFERENCES	
	Catherine Linton	Linton Heathcliff
• fair hair	•	•
•	•	•
•		
•		

4 Mrs Dean plays an important role as information provider for Lockwood (and consequently, for us, the reader) and for the characters in the story. In Chapter Fifteen, she tells the children about their past. She answers young Linton's questions on their way to Wuthering Heights. In pairs, prepare her answers to his questions. Then act out the dialogue. Take it in turns to be Linton and Mrs Dean.

5 Can you explain the paradox of Nelly's consideration at the end of the chapter, 'Heathcliff's selfishness will make him treat the boy (Linton) well'?

CAE (6) **For questions 1-8, read the text. Use the words in capitals to form one word that fits in the space in the text. The exercise begins with an example (0).**

Wuthering Heights (1939) is director William Wyler's tale of doomed and tragic love, (**0**) ...conflicting........ passions and revenge. It is considered one of Hollywood's most romantic classics. Filmed with	CONFLICT
(**1**) .... beauty, it is the first film	HAUNT
(**2**) .... of Emily Brontë's wildly passionate best-selling literary masterpiece.	DRAMA
The 1939 film was a critical success, earning 8 Academy Award (**3**) .... in what is often called 'the	NOMINATE
greatest year in (**4**) .... picture history.' The nominations included Best Picture, Best	MOVE
(**5**) .... Actress and Best Director. The film's	SUPPORT
musical score by Alfred Newman is (**6**)	FORGET
The leading actors began work on the film under (**7**) .... circumstances, including the fact	MISERY
that both had their own lovers in England. For both its major stars, however, the film turned out to be (**8**)	ADVANTAGE

 INTERNET PROJECT

Connect to the Internet and go to www.blackcat-cideb.com or www.cideb.it. Insert the title or part of the title of the book into our search engine.

Open the page for *Wuthering Heights*. Click on the internet project link. Go down the page until you find the title of this book and click on the relevant link for this project.

Find out more about the film versions of *Wuthering Heights*.

▶ When was the first film of the book made?

▶ Try and read some more reviews of the films. Which is your favourite version?

▶ Try and watch one of the versions of the films. Is it different from the book?

So the cousins grew up separately — Cathy at the Grange, and Linton at the Heights — and they never saw each other, though she asked about him often. One day, when Cathy was sixteen years old, she asked her father if she could go walking on the moors with me. He said that she could, but that we must not go far.

Cathy ran ahead of me as soon as we were beyond the park gates. 'Miss Cathy! Slow down!' I cried, but it was no use. She ran, laughing, and I had to run after her. 'Miss Cathy! That's far enough! We must turn back home now!' I cried, when I saw that she was going too far and in the direction of Wuthering Heights.

'Oh just let's go a little further, Nelly!' she called back to me, and she continued to run. When I got to the top of the next hill, I saw her far below me, talking to someone. We were now on the edge of Heathcliff's property, and I recognised the tall figure by her as Heathcliff. 'Miss Cathy! Come away! Come back now!' I cried, but she ignored me, and I had to run down the hill after her.

'Hello, Nelly!' said Heathcliff. 'Come to the Heights for a little while. I want young Catherine to meet Linton.'

'Oh no! Her father will be very angry with me if I let her go to the Heights. Please, Miss Cathy, come home now!'

Heathcliff took hold of my arm and pulled me along towards Wuthering Heights. 'Don't be silly, Nelly,' he said. 'What harm can it do?'

'I'm sure that you have a bad reason for inviting her,' said I.

'Nonsense,' said he. 'I'll tell you my reason. I want the two cousins to fall in love and marry. You know that young Catherine will have nothing when her father dies. If she marries Linton, she will be the mistress of Thrushcross Grange.'

'Perhaps he will not live long enough to marry,' said I. 'And if he dies, young Catherine will inherit the Grange.'

'You are wrong there, Nelly. If Linton dies, I shall inherit the Grange. I am his closest relative. No. It would be far better if they married.'

We went into the house, and there was Linton. He had grown tall and graceful. 'Linton, is it really you?' asked Cathy, kissing him. 'How tall you are! You are taller than I am!' Then she turned to Heathcliff and said, 'So you are my uncle. How strange that you live so near us and yet we never see you. From now on, I will come every day!'

'Your father wouldn't like that,' said Heathcliff. 'He doesn't like me. If you want to come here to visit sometimes, you will have to keep it a secret from your father. He would not allow you to come.'

'Then Linton must come to see us at the Grange,' said Cathy.

'Oh, I couldn't walk so far,' said Linton. 'It would kill me. No. You must come here, Miss Catherine. Not every day, but once or twice a week.'

Heathcliff looked at his son with contempt. 'You see what a weakling [1] he is, Nelly,' said he. 'Soon she will see it herself and want nothing to do with him. Now if it were Hareton, things would be different. I often wish that Hareton were my son. But no — he is Hindley's son, and I've made it my business to treat him just as Hindley treated me. He has had no lessons. He cannot read or write. He works on the farm like a servant. Young Catherine will never look at him! I have seen him looking at her, and I know how he feels, because I suffered it all before him!'

---

1. **weakling** : weak and pathetic person.

When we returned to the Grange, we told my master about our visit to Wuthering Heights. He explained to Catherine why he did not wish her to go there, and she promised not to go again. The next day, however, she sent a note to Linton. I did not know it at the time. In fact, many months passed before I realised that Cathy was writing regularly to Linton, sending him presents and receiving presents in return. One day I found her secret store [1] of letters from him. The first letters were short and timid, but the later ones were long love letters. I suspected that Heathcliff had helped — maybe even forced — his son to write them. I confronted [2] Cathy and made her promise to write no more letters to her cousin. I threatened to tell her father, and she promised that she would not write again. For some time after that she was very sad and spent hours crying alone in her room. Then a letter arrived for her from Heathcliff. In it he said that Linton had fallen ill, because he was so unhappy that Catherine did not write to him anymore. Heathcliff said that he was going away for a week. Surely, he said, she would come and visit her cousin while he — Heathcliff — was away.

It was winter then, and my master had been ill for some months. At first the doctor had said it was just a bad cold, but then my master seemed to get weaker, and I feared that he would die. In January, I too fell ill with a fever, just about the time that Cathy received Heathcliff's letter. I thought that she must have been very lonely for those weeks when both her father and I were ill in our beds. Later, however, I discovered that she had not been entirely alone. A few days after I recovered, Cathy told me that she had a

---

1. **store** : things put away in a special place.
2. **confronted** : faced her about the problem so she could not avoid it.

headache and would go to bed early. Two hours later, I went up to her room to see if she wanted something to eat, but she was not there. I waited by her bedroom window, and after another hour I saw her return from the moors on her pony.

When I confronted her, she told me everything. Every evening for the three weeks I had been ill, she had gone to Wuthering Heights to see her cousin. Sometimes they had passed pleasant hours together laughing and talking, but more often Linton had been peevish and irritable. He and Catherine had argued more than once. On other occasions Linton argued with Hareton. Hareton seemed jealous that Catherine came to see Linton. He often tried to engage her in conversation, but she was not interested in talking to him. These evenings at Wuthering Heights, therefore, were not all happy ones, and yet she continued to go. Once she had told Linton that she would not visit him anymore, since he was so irritable with her and did not seem to enjoy her company. Then he begged her to come again. He said he knew that he was weak and peevish and bad-tempered, and he was very sorry. He said it was because he was ill, and he begged her to forgive him.

The next day, I told my master all that Cathy had told me. It made him very sad and worried, but finally he agreed to let the cousins meet on the moors once a week to walk or ride together. Because of Linton's health, they could not do this until the warm weather came. When finally they did meet, I accompanied Cathy to the meeting. Linton looked even weaker and more sickly than he had the last time I saw him, though he said he felt stronger. He was too weak to walk or ride, and he fell asleep for some of the time we were together. He often coughed, and once I saw blood on his lips. I was certain that he was lying about his health, and I could not imagine why he would do so. However, just before we left him, he said something that seemed to explain his strange behaviour.

'Miss Catherine, if you see my father, and he asks you how I was, please do not tell him that I slept or that I was silent and stupid,' he begged anxiously.

'Is your father unkind to you, Master Linton?' I asked.

'He would be angry, and I am afraid of making him angry,' said the poor weakling. 'And do please come again next Thursday. Please come to see me here again!'

As we rode away, Catherine looked anxious and disappointed. 'Nelly, he acts as if he only wants to see me to stop his father from being angry with him!' she said at last.

The following Thursday, we went to the same place. Linton was waiting there, looking paler than ever.

'Linton,' said Catherine sternly. 'I know that you do not really wish to see me. Why do you make me come here, if you do not wish it? My father is dying. I want to spend every moment by his bedside. I will not come here again.'

'Please Catherine,' he began, but then his cough interrupted him. 'Don't be angry with me. It is not my fault. If I betray you, it is because I have no choice. I am so afraid!' He began coughing again and leaned upon [1] her arm. 'It's no use. Please take me back to Wuthering Heights. I cannot walk alone.'

'Linton, you know my father has forbidden me to go to Wuthering Heights. We must call a servant to take you home.'

'There is no one in the house except my father, and I am so afraid of him,' sobbed Linton. 'Please, Catherine, just help me back to the house.'

---

1. **leaned upon** : supported himself on.

Catherine agreed and walked to Wuthering Heights, with her arm around Linton's waist. When we reached the door, she tried to move away from him, but he grasped her arm and said, 'Take me into the sitting room to my chair, please, Catherine. I will fall over if I try to walk alone.'

Just then, Heathcliff appeared from behind the house and grasped my arm. 'Come on, Nelly. Into the house,' he said, pushing me forward. As soon as we were in the sitting room, Heathcliff locked the door.

'What are you doing?' cried Catherine.

'I'm going to keep you here until you marry my son!' said Heathcliff.

'I'm not afraid of you!' cried Catherine, starting to scratch and bite his hand in her attempt to get the key. 'You can't keep me here! My father will be worried about me. Let me go home now, and I will marry Linton tomorrow.'

'Yes,' said Heathcliff. 'You will marry Linton tomorrow, but you will not go home tonight. I'm very glad to hear that your father will be worried. It makes me all the more determined to keep you here!'

Catherine bit his hand hard, but he grasped her arm and slapped her face several times. Then he took us upstairs and locked us in a bedroom. We looked for a way to escape, but the windows were too narrow. We were imprisoned, and there was nothing we could do. The next morning, Heathcliff opened the door and took Catherine away, then he locked the door again. I was left alone in that room for five days. The only person I saw in all that time was Hareton, who brought me food but said nothing. I was left alone to worry about what was happening to my young mistress, and how my poor master would bear it when he heard all.

Go back to the text

1 The story moves forward several years and Cathy is 16. Complete the sentences with appropriate phrases.

1 If Cathy went to Wuthering Heights, her father...
2 Heathcliff wants Cathy to come to Wuthering Heights to...
3 By marrying Linton Heathcliff, Catherine will...
4 If Linton dies before marrying Catherine, Heathcliff will...
5 Heathcliff tells Cathy that she can come to Wuthering Heights provided she...

2 Why do you think Heathcliff wishes Hareton were his son?

3 Which of these statements do you agree with? Discuss your views with other students in small groups.

1 Heathcliff is using Linton to achieve his aims.
2 Linton loves Catherine.
3 Linton maintains a relationship with Catherine in order to satisfy his father.
4 Catherine is genuinely fond of Linton Heathcliff.
5 Linton did not expect his father to abduct Catherine and Mrs Dean.
6 Catherine has no intention of marrying Linton.

4 What do you think will happen in the next chapter? Decide whether these events are probable or unlikely. Compare ideas with a partner.

	Event	Probable or unlikely?
1	Catherine and Mrs Dean manage to escape	
2	Mrs Dean manages to escape with Hareton's help	
3	Linton Heathcliff convinces Heathcliff to let them go	
4	Mrs Dean is allowed to go but Catherine isn't	
5	Catherine manages to escape with Linton's help	

CHAPTER 17

On the fifth day, Zillah unlocked the door. She was surprised to find me there and said that everyone in the village thought that Catherine and I had got lost on the moor. I asked her where Catherine was, but she said she knew nothing. Mr Heathcliff, she said, was out.

Downstairs, I found young Linton in the sitting room.

'Where is Miss Catherine?' I demanded.

'She is upstairs, locked in her room,' said Linton. 'Yesterday she was allowed downstairs, but she cried and screamed so much that we had to lock her up again. She gives me a headache. Father says that she hates me. She wants me to die. But she is my wife now, so it is shameful that she should hate me.'

'Do you know where the key is?'

'Yes, but I won't tell you where it is. I won't let her run away to Thrushcross Grange. I am her husband now. She should love me more than she loves her father, even if he is dying.'

'What?' I cried. 'Is my master dying?'

'The doctors say so,' said Linton.

I thought it best to leave Wuthering Heights before Heathcliff returned. Then I could send a group of men from the Grange to rescue my young lady. When I arrived at Thrushcross Grange, I ran straight to my master's room. How changed he was, even in those few days! He was very pale and thin. I told him that Heathcliff had forced us to stay at Wuthering Heights and that Catherine was now married to Linton. I did not tell him the worst details, because I did not want to distress him more than necessary.

That evening, Catherine came to Thrushcross Grange. She had persuaded Linton to unlock her door and had run all the way from Wuthering Heights. By the time she arrived, however, her father was very weak indeed. He gazed at her with loving eyes and said that he was going to join her mother. He died peacefully a few hours later.

The next day, my master was buried beside his wife in the churchyard on the moor. The following evening, Heathcliff came to Thrushcross Grange. He walked in without knocking at the door. He was the master now.

'I have come to take young Catherine home,' he said. 'There will be no more running away. She is Linton's wife, and she belongs at his side.'

'Why not let Catherine and Linton live here?' I asked.

'I am seeking [1] a tenant for the Grange,' said Heathcliff. 'Besides, I want my children to live with me. Get ready, Catherine. Come home to your husband.'

'I will!' said Catherine. 'Linton is all I have to love in the world now, and you cannot make us hate each other! I know he has a bad nature, but I forgive him! I know he loves me, and therefore I will love him. Mr Heathcliff, you have nobody to love you; however miserable you make us, we will have the comfort of knowing that you are more miserable still. You are miserable, are you not? Lonely, like the devil, and envious like him? Nobody loves you. Nobody will cry when you die. I wouldn't be you!'

She ran upstairs to pack her things. Heathcliff stood by the fire, looking at the portraits of my master and mistress. 'I'll take her portrait back to Wuthering Heights,' he said. 'I don't need it, but...' He turned away from the fire with a strange smile on his face. 'I'll tell you what I did yesterday! I asked the man who was

---

1. **seeking** : looking for.

digging Edgar Linton's grave to remove the earth off her coffin [1] lid, and I opened it. When I saw her face — it is still her face — I thought I would stay there forever, but the man told me that the air would damage her face. So I covered her up again. But then I removed one side of her coffin. Not the side next to Linton, damn him! I paid the man some money and he agreed to bury me beside her, on the side where her coffin is open, and to leave that side of my coffin open too, so that, by the time Edgar Linton gets to us, he won't know which is which!'

'You are very wicked, Mr Heathcliff!' I cried. 'Were you not ashamed to disturb the dead?'

'I have not disturbed her; she disturbs me! I have a strong faith in ghosts. I am convinced that they can and do exist among us! Every night for eighteen years she has disturbed me — until last night. Last night I dreamt that I was tranquil, lying dead beside her, with my cheek frozen against hers. The first time she came to me was the night after she was buried. I went to the graveyard. It was snowing. I dug down to her coffin in a rage, filled with the desire to have her in my arms again. But, just as I was pulling at the coffin lid, I heard a sigh from the edge of the grave, and I knew that her spirit was there, not below me but on the earth. I felt consoled at once, and I stopped tearing at the coffin lid. I climbed out of the grave and filled it in with earth. Since then I have often felt her presence, but I have never seen her. It is intolerable torture to know she is near but not to see her! She has been a devil to me these eighteen years, killing me slowly, torturing me to death!'

Mr Heathcliff fell silent and wiped [2] the sweat from his

---

1. **coffin** : wooden box in which a dead body is placed.
2. **wiped** : removed.

forehead. Then I heard my young lady coming down the stairs with her bags. 'Goodbye, Ellen!' she said, and kissed my cheek. Her lips felt as cold as ice. 'Come and see me soon!'

'Mrs Dean cannot come to see you,' said Heathcliff sternly. 'She will be busy here, taking care of my tenant. Do not come to Wuthering Heights, Ellen! If I want to talk to you, I will come here.'

Then he led Catherine out of the house and off to Wuthering Heights.

I have not seen my young lady since that day. All I know of life at Wuthering Heights is what Zillah tells me when I meet her in the village. Zillah told me that, the morning after she came to the house, Catherine asked Heathcliff to send for the doctor, because Linton was dying. Heathcliff said he did not care and would not spend money on doctors for Linton. Catherine nursed Linton alone. Heathcliff had told Zillah not to interfere, and Zillah, being a selfish stupid woman, obeyed him. Catherine was up day and night with her dying husband. Sometimes Zillah saw her sitting on the stairs at night, weeping. But she never tried to comfort my poor young lady: her master had told her not to interfere, and she obeyed her master's orders.

Finally, young Linton died. Catherine was ill for two weeks after his death. When she recovered, Heathcliff showed her Linton's will.[1] Linton had left everything to his father. Heathcliff must have forced him to write that will. Catherine was left penniless, completely dependent upon her father-in-law.

Thus ended Mrs Dean's story.

---

1. **will** : legal document stating to whom your possessions are to be given after your death.

Go back to the text

1 Go back to the predictions you made at the end of the last chapter. Were you right?

2 In what way does Edgar's mourning for Catherine and his state of mind before dying compare with Heathcliff's?

3 Heathcliff's disturbance of Catherine's grave has shocked generations of readers. Why do you think he did it?

4 What is your opinion of Catherine's behaviour in this chapter?

5 Why will Catherine be economically dependent on her father-in-law, Heathcliff?

CAE **6** Heathcliff tells us two gothic tales, stories popular in the late eighteenth and early nineteenth centuries. For questions 1-11, complete the following article by writing each missing word in each space. Use only one word for each space. The exercise begins with an example (0).

The gothic novel was a literary genre that belonged (0) ..to.......... Romanticism and began in Britain with *The Castle of Otranto* (1764) by Horace Walpole. It depended for its effect (1) .... the pleasing terror it induced in the reader. It is the predecessor (2) .... modern horror fiction and has produced the common definition of 'gothic' (3) .... being connected to the dark and horrific.

The term 'gothic' came to (4) .... applied to the literary genre because it dealt (5) .... emotional extremes and dark themes, and because it found (6) .... most natural settings in the buildings of this style — castles, mansions and monasteries.

It was Ann Radcliffe (7) .... created the gothic novel in its now-standard form. Radcliffe introduced the figure of the gothic villain, (8) .... developed into the Byronic hero. Her novels, beginning (9) .... *The Mysteries of Udolpho* (1794), were best-sellers, and virtually everyone (10) .... English society was reading them. Mary Shelley's *Frankenstein* (1818) is undoubtedly (11) .... of the most important literary triumphs of this period.

CHAPTER 18

1802. In the second week of January I was feeling stronger, so I rode over to Wuthering Heights to tell my landlord that I would leave Thrushcross Grange. Hareton Earnshaw let me in. I took more notice of him this time. He was a handsome lad, but his manner was very rough. I asked if Mr Heathcliff were at home. He told me that Heathcliff was out but would return for dinner. I said that I would wait for him. Catherine was in the sitting room preparing some vegetables for dinner. She seemed sadder and less spirited than before. She did not greet me but went on with her task as if I were not there.

When Heathcliff arrived, I noticed that he was thinner and had a restless anxious expression.

'I am going to London, Mr Heathcliff,' said I, 'and I will not return to Thrushcross Grange. You can find another tenant for October.'

'Oh, indeed!' said he. 'But you must pay your rent till October, sir, as we agreed.'

'Of course,' I replied, irritated by his manner. 'I'll pay you now if you like.'

Riding away from Wuthering Heights, I thought what a strange romantic fairy tale it would have been if Mrs Linton Heathcliff and I had fallen in love, and I had taken her away with me from this lonely place to the lively atmosphere of London!

The following September, as I was going to visit a friend in the North, I realised that my journey took me close to Thrushcross Grange. I had a sudden impulse to spend the night there. After all, I had paid the rent: it was mine until October. I stopped the carriage in the village and told my driver to sleep at the inn and be ready to drive on in the morning. Then I walked to the Grange. When I got there, however, I found a strange woman in the kitchen. I told her who I was and asked her to prepare a room for me, then I asked her where Mrs Dean was.

'She lives up at Wuthering Heights now,' said the woman. I decided to go to Wuthering Heights to see Mrs Dean. The sun was setting and the moon was rising as I left the park. When I reached Wuthering Heights, I noticed that the doors and windows were open, and there were flowers in the garden. That is an improvement! I thought. As I approached the door, I heard voices from within.

'No, no, no!' said a voice as sweet as a silver bell. 'Read it again, and this time with no mistakes.'

'Kiss me first!' said a deeper voice.

'Not until you have read it perfectly!'

I looked in and saw Catherine and Hareton by the window, with their heads bent close together over a book. Hareton was handsome, clean, and well-dressed, and his face glowed with pleasure. Her face was full of gentle tender affection. Seeing it, I felt sad at the thought of what I had missed.

When Hareton had read the passage through with no mistakes, Catherine kissed him and said, 'Let's go for our walk now.' I did not want to interrupt them, so I hid behind the door until they were gone. When they were out of the gate, I looked into the sitting room again and saw my old friend Nelly Dean sitting by the fire, sewing. She saw me and leapt to her feet. 'Mr Lockwood! Why didn't you tell us you were coming! Thrushcross Grange will not be ready for you!'

'Don't worry,' said I. 'I have been to Thrushcross Grange, and the housekeeper is preparing a room for me now. But tell me: why aren't you at Thrushcross Grange, Mrs Dean?'